I0549181

Also by Joan Byrd
From Indigo Sea Press

The All My Tomorrows Series:

A New Beginning

Love Finds a Way

Today, Tomorrow and Always

Untold Stories of Jesus

The Box in the Attic

The Good Seed—the Bad Seed

The Shadow of the Moon Rider

indigoseapress.com

THE SEED HAS BEEN SOWN

BY

JOAN BYRD

Deep Indigo Books
Published by Indigo Sea Press
Winston-Salem

Deep Indigo Books
Indigo Sea Press
PO Box 26701
Winston-Salem, NC 27114

This book is a work of fiction. Names, characters, locations and events are either a product of the author's imagination, fictitious or used fictitiously. Any resemblance to any event, locale or person, living or dead, is purely coincidental.

Copyright 2020 by Joan Byrd
All rights reserved, including the right of reproduction in whole or part in any format.
First Deep Indigo Books edition published
May, 2020
Deep Indigo Books, Moon Sailor and all production design are trademarks of Indigo Sea Press, used under license.

For information regarding bulk purchases of this book, digital purchase and special discounts, please contact the publisher at indigoseapress@gmail.com

Cover design by Pan Morelli
Manufactured in the United States of America
ISBN 978-1-63066-503-6

DEDICATION

Prayer is a powerful and wonderful thing! The more I dedicate my time in prayer, the closer I get to my holy family! There are two places in my home where I find peace, and that is where I pray, morning and night. My morning altar is just outside my upstairs window, when it's still dark outside. Our security light sits at the end of our driveway and there are trees that block it. Yet, the light shines in the middle of a cross, that glows and sparkles as it reflects the love of Jesus. This is where I heard God say to me: "save my babies!" Patrick and I knew he wanted me to write a book about abortion and to help women decide to keep god's gift!

I dedicate this book to all the unborn babies God has lovingly created and placed their little soul into their bodies, as soon as the seed was sown! God's special gift, the child he had planned to be born, even before the beginning of time!

—Joan Byrd

Chapter 1

Rebecca stared down at her solo she had wanted so badly. She had thought her good friend Nancy was sure to get it. Christmas was always a special time for the eighteen-year-old college freshman and even though her shyness was her greatest handicap, the one thing she excelled at was singing.

"The voice of an angel," her father had told her the moment she lifted her small voice in song at the early age of two. He was quite proud of his beautiful talented daughter.

Lost in her enter thoughts, Rebecca had not noticed everyone from choir practice had left except her and Mr. Spangler, the choir director, who touched her shoulder gently.

"Rebecca, gather your things. It is getting late and the sun is dropping fast." Mr. Spangler smiled as he zipped up his music case and pulled out his car's keys. "Need a lift?" Knowing Rebecca lived only one block from church and walked to choir practice since it let out before dark, he knew his offer would be refused graciously by the beautiful shy girl. Besides, the town of Maglen was one of the smallest and safest towns in the state of North Carolina. The biggest thing to happen in the small rural town was the building of Maglen University, known for its outstanding courses, the arts among the greatest achievements.

"That is most kind of you Mr. Spangler, but I will be find. Thank you anyway." Rebecca followed him out the church door and pulling her wool scarf tighter around her neck to ward off the winter wind, she made her way quickly down the street to home, as she had done many times before.

Knowing the house would be empty of family members, Rebecca was glad for the last rays of sunlight that seen her safely home and inside. Locking the door behind her, she switched on the overhead light in the entrance hall and picked

1

up the mail she had gathered earlier from the mailbox that sit at the end of their long driveway.

Rebecca had always felt safe in her warm big farmhouse with the wrap around porch, even with her parents away at a cattle sale. It wasn't unusual for a farm this size to be on the outskirts of this rural town. With the Methodist church sitting at the edge of town, the city road instantly becomes a country road and the Bradford's farm was only the first to dot the country farm lands.

Rebecca went through the stack of mail, a Good Housekeeping, her mother ordered and enjoyed, The Farm Journal, her father's favorite, early Christmas cards from close relatives, a couple bills, that always seem to come too soon, and a post card, picturing a funny looking bull with a Santa hat atop his horns. Laughing softly, Rebecca turned the card over and recognized her mother's handwriting.

"Got here safe, despite your daddy's fast driving. I know we are in the right place from the 'sweet smell'. Keep the home fires glowing. Daddy and I send our love. Stay safe! See you on Monday. Mama."

Rebecca carefully laid down the mail along with her Christmas Cantata book, and removed her heavy coat and scarf, then placed them inside the hall closet. She checked her watch and knew she had only a few short hours left before turning in for the night. Classes came early on the campus during the weekdays, so Rebecca made it her rule to get up every morning at the exact same hour, even on the weekend.

Voice and singing were her favorite and very first class in the mornings at 8:00a.m. Rebecca really loved and respected her music professor, Mrs. Darlene Clayborn, who's kindness and exceptional manners was far different from Eric Shields, her History professor. Mr. Shields prided himself in knowing history and to be his student, you had to take his words for "gospel." Eric Shields was all business, with penetrating eyes and he rarely showed any emotion. Even though Mr. Shields was quite handsome, he never smiled.

Rebecca had chosen History because it always held great interest to her ever since she learned at an early age in Sunday school, how life had begun by the loving God she chose to serve. Rebecca was expecting a teacher who was open to all history, especially American History and Religious History. So, she was not prepared for Professor Shields and his outspoken belief, or the correct word, Rebecca thought, was his unbelief.

She had signed up for one year in History, just to see if she like the course, but the homework Professor Shields sent home for his students, was overwhelming at best, even for a straight A student like Rebecca.

She switched on the television set and turned it to her favorite show that had just started. She knew she wouldn't have time to watch "Touch by An Angel" so she set the recorder and planned to watch it Saturday night. She had a paper to finish for History class tomorrow.

Rebecca went to the kitchen and poured herself a tall glass of milk and took two cookies from the old blue cookie jar, then she spread her books out on the kitchen table and mumbled to herself.

"Why would Mr. Shields hold a class on Saturday? Being in his class five days a week is more than enough for me!" Rebecca clicked her pen on her paper, breaking the stillness that surrounded her. His words came back in her mind as she tried to concentrate on her history theme paper.

"Class, choose a subject and a time in history that is of interest to you. I want each and everyone to turn in your paper this Saturday. To get a passing grade this semester, you 'must' attend class this Saturday, 1:00p.m. sharp!"

Rebecca smiled down at her title. "He Walked in Galilee". She yawned, glad that she was almost finished, as she wrote down the last words and spoke softly to herself.

"I wonder what Mr. Shields will say when he reads my

3

words about the one I love most in this world? If he should ask me why I chose this subject and time in history, I will simply reply, this is what interest me. There is no greater subject than Jesus and no greater time than when He walked this earth, teaching us how to live."

The big grandfather clock in the front hall struck nine as she stacked up the theme paper and slipped it carefully onto a binder. Rebecca reverently touched the cross hanging around her neck as she smiled upward and spoke softly.

"Thank you, Lord, for another beautiful day, for keeping my voice clear and strong for practice, and for helping me through another class with Professor Shields." Switching off the kitchen light, Rebecca started to walk from the kitchen when she froze and listened carefully. Somewhere in the house, she had heard a soft creak. "It's probably just our old heart pine floors expanding with the sudden drop in temperature after the sun gave way to darkness."

After putting her books away Rebecca started upstairs when she heard the creak again, only, this time, a little louder. She stopped on the stairs, her heart racing with second thoughts.

Maybe their collie Maggie had found a way inside from her cold doghouse and she had wondered upstairs and was waiting for a treat. Reaching the top landing, Rebecca walked to the hall window and looked out at the doghouse. She could plainly see Maggie curled up asleep just inside. Suddenly the phone rang out and Rebecca twirled around, holding in her scream. Without hesitation, she raced inside her bedroom, shut the door, then grabbed the receiver,

"Hello." She said, as her eyes scanned her dark room, found the desk lamp and switched it on.

"Hi Bec, this is Nancy! How did practice go this evening? I'm sorry I missed it, but this stupid cold is just about to get the best of me. I'm glad I don't have classes tomorrow." The girl friend stiffed.

"Hello Nancy. I missed singing next to you tonight." Rebecca felt a little silly for getting so frightened over the sounds old houses made. "Practice went well and Mr. Spangler gave out the cantata solos." She knew it was not right to brag over getting the prettiest solo in the Christmas Cantata nor did she wish to hurt her best friend's feelings, so she wouldn't say who got them.

"I talked to Martha Fuller earlier this evening. She called me when she got back home and said you got the solo, The Little Lamb." Nancy coughed, then blew her nose. "I think that is wonderful, Bec! That solo was written for your beautiful voice. It's one of the prettiest Christmas songs I have heard and I could tell when we all rehearsed it, it moved you deeply."

"Yes, the words telling how Jesus was the little lamb sent by His Father to save us. Nancy, I hope you are not too disappointed that you didn't get a solo. You always sing your solos so lovely, they make me cry." Rebecca meant every word. "Mr. Spangler gave Jane Cook the other solo, but it was for an alto."

"Rebecca Bradford, don't you go worrying about my feelings, dear friend. I am perfectly happy to sit this year's solos out and just lift my voice with the choir." Nancy laughed, then coughed. "Besides Bec, no one else could do The Little Lamb as beautiful as you and that's because you have always been Jesus' little lamb."

"I love you too, Nancy." Rebecca yawned. "I finally finished my theme paper, now I am ready for professor know-it-all!"

"I'm glad I chose nursing." Nancy shook, remembering just passing the serious looking professor in the halls at the college. "That man gives me the creeps, the way he stares right through you. And making your class come in on Saturday, what a jerk! At least it's not Sunday!"

"I believe he would think twice before asking the class to

5

meet on Sunday. He knows most of the students are Christians and we know God's Sabbath is Holy and a day of rest and praising the Lord." Rebecca felt her eyes getting heavy as she yawned again. "And I agree with you concerning Professor Shields giving you the creeps. I'm seriously considering dropping his class next year." Her eyes fell on her bedside clock and noticed it was already 10:00p.m. "I'm sorry Nancy, but I really must turn in. I have chores in the morning before I'm due in class horrible." Her friend laughed.

"Then off to bed with you and I will say a little prayer that your dreams be free of Professor know-it-all."

"Thanks Nancy, I can do without nightmares." Saying goodnight, Rebecca slipped out of her shirt and jeans and started to put on her nightgown when she heard the familiar creak, directly behind her. Afraid to turn around, she started to put her gown on a second time when a hand touched her shoulder.

"Are you going to leave those underwear on to sleep in…Rebecca?" the deep voice of a man filled the silence as his other hand reached over and switched off the desk lamp.

Chapter 2

Rebecca was overcome by sudden fear, unlike anything she has ever felt. She found it hard to breathe as she could feel her body shaking uncontrollable.

"Relax Rebecca, you have nothing to fear from me." His voice came softly in her ear. "I knew you were alone and I wanted to see if you were alright."

"I…I am fine." She swallowed, trying to make out the man's voice. "Really, you can go, I will be fine by myself."

"I consider myself your…guardian angel, Rebecca." His hand rubbed her hair slowly. "You believe in angels, don't you?"

"By faith, yes, I truly believe in angels." She closed her eyes and wished that her real guardian angel could intervene and change the course of this man's choice. "An angel would not slip into someone's home and cut out the lights, nor would they frighten a child of God."

"You are such a good girl, Rebecca." There was a hint of mockery in his tone. "Someday you will make some lucky man a beautiful bride."

"Are you a good person? What is your name?" she stalled for time.

"I know the Bible well child, and my name, well let's just say, you know me very well." He rubbed his hand down her neck, her back, then over her buttocks. "Mumm, you have certainly been blessed Rebecca. Soon I will be blessed with the pleasure of your young body."

"Please, don't rape me." Rebecca whispered, her fear growing stronger. "The man I marry should be my first."

"Rebecca, you are so pure and innocent. A devoted Christian girl and a virgin, at least for now." A sneer came in his tone. "Not to mention, a voice of an angel."

"Please, who are you and why are you doing this?" her voice trembled.

"I've been observing you for some time, Rebecca. Such beautiful blonde hair." Again, his hand gentle touched her hair. "If it starts to fade with age, you can buy the same shade, in the local drugstore."

This man seemed to know conversations she had made with several men she knew, Rebecca thought. So far, he repeated the words of her preacher, the local pharmacist, their handy man, Buck, who live on the farm, and even her own daddy.

His hand moved down her back and stopped at her bra. He unsnapped the hooks and slid the straps down her shoulder. Cupping each breast in his hands, he pulled her up next to him. Rebecca could feel the large swell in his pants and she closed her eyes, fearing the worse. His breathing grew heavy as he spoke next to her ear.

"God, Rebecca, your breast is even more luscious than I dreamed." His, slow moving fingers made her fell sick as she pleaded

"Please stop!" his fingers pulled at her nipples as he whispered breathlessly.

"Rebecca, does not the Bible say, you are not to turn a stranger away?"

"But, you are no stranger. You yourself, said I knew you well." Rebecca fault back the fear swelling in her body. "If you were a stranger, I would gladly give you some food or a warm coat."

"My beautiful girl, it is not food or a warm coat I desire." He pulled her panties to the floor with expert speed. "It's your body Rebecca, I must have it! I have long for it for a long time! You cannot refuse me! You won't 'pass' the test, acting so cold toward me. You do want to pass, don't you Rebecca?"

"A fifth man." She thought, as chills ran down her naked body. "This time it was Professor Shields, God forbid!"

Suddenly, Rebecca realized he had, at some point, removed his clothes, when he lifted her up into his arms, keeping his face hidden from the moonlight coming dimly through her curtains.

"This time, you cannot refuse my lift, Rebecca." He carried her to the bed and laid her down. She still could not make out his features in the dark room and could only tell he was tall, well built with dark hair. The description could have fit either of the five men and now a sixth, her choir director.

"So beautiful lying there, so tempting, my little lamb." He laughed softly as he fell over her grabbing her arms and pinning them down.

"Please, please...don't do this!" she could barely make out his eyes. "If you stop and leave now, I will not tell anyone!"

"Rebecca, Rebecca." He squeezed her arms as he got up next to her ear. "What can you tell anyone? You do not know who I am. You don't want to be a disgraced child." He kissed her neck and breast. "And besides..." he spoke harshly as he slid deep inside her, causing a sharp pain to engulf her. "you belong to me, Rebecca! Just relax, and enjoy this beautiful feeling." He moaned in deep satisfaction and she felt the warm liquid run inside her. Her rapist laid still for a minute, then his hand wrapped around her throat.

"Say nothing to no one Rebecca and I will not hurt you." He laughed, sending a cold sweat up her neck. "Who knows, I might need you again."

Rebecca broke down in sobs when he released her throat and stood up to get dressed.

"If you try and guess who I am, you could ruin many lives by guessing the wrong man. I know what your thoughts are. There are six of us and each man has a wife or a girlfriend. Most of them have children or, at least, one little girl." He moved to the door and glanced back. "Don't call the sheriff beautiful, besides, the phone lines are dead. I couldn't allow you to do something stupid." Slipping out, he closed her door and she could hear his footsteps on the wooden stairs, then somewhere downstairs, a door closed.

JOAN BYRD

Pulling the covers tight around her neck, Rebecca cried herself to sleep.

Chapter 3

Rebecca could fell the warm sunlight on her face and knew she had not set her clock. " Perhaps it had only been a bad dream," she thought, "and when I look under these sheets, I will be in my gown." To her great disappointment, it was not a dream when she noticed she was naked under the white sheets. Sitting up nervously, she looked around the familiar room. Nothing had been moved and the only thing out of place was her nightgown and underwear lying on the floor where her attacker dropped them.

Rebecca climbed quickly from her bed and went to the bathroom to take a hot shower, to wash away the unwelcomed rapist. As the water ran over her, tears once again filled her blue eyes. She went through the motions of getting dressed and as she was putting on her shoes, her attention fell on the bed. She walked over and yanked the sheets from the bed so she could put them in the washer. As she gathered them up in her arms, Rebecca heard something metal hit the floor and roll.

She realized immediately her attacker had lost something. So, throwing the sheets aside, Rebecca got down on her knees and searched under her bed, the bedside table, then looked under her dresser. Something silver caught her eye and she reached under and brought out an unusual ring. Looking closer, it appeared to be a cross, lying on its side and engraved on the inside was initials, KOTFC. Rebecca could not recall seeing either of her six suspects wearing the odd ring.

Rebecca went about doing her chores. Milking the cow, feeding the chickens and Maggie, their collie. She made sure the cows in the pasture had plenty of hay and water, then she checked her watch. There were only two hours left before her history class started, so she decided to go to her neighbor, who lived a mile down the road, borrow their phone and report the

11

outage. Rebecca wanted to get back as close to normal as possible when her parents returned on Monday. This was one secret she wished not to share with anyone, even her best friends, Nancy and Brook, her favorite first cousin.

Rape victims always seem to be treated like they were the ones to blame. Something they had done that drove the rapist to do his horrible act. No, she would not tell anyone and try to bury it deep inside with a lot of praying to the one true friend she could turn to. Her loving Lord and Savior.

Rebecca grabbed her car keys and looked up at her reflection in the hall mirror. She still looked the same, nothing on the outside showed what her inward emotions were feeling. Somehow, with God's help, she would keep this secret that no one else knew. Then she could almost feel his presents behind her, and hear him whisper softly in her ear

"But Rebecca, my beautiful blonde child, you with the voice of an angel, I know…I know!"

Victoria Sinclair's smooth voice told the evening news with calm emotions, that drew many viewers to watch her. She was as pretty as she was talented. Victoria could tell serious news with drama, be warm and loving over a sweet moving story or her happy smile could lighten the hearts of everyone who watched her tell a funny bit that happened around town.

The six o'clock news was over directly at 7:00p.m. and Miss Sinclair need not return until her 11:00 news hour started. Being a good reporter, Victoria would arrive back at the station at least one hour before the news to go over everything that was scheduled for the evening news.

"Your usual Saturday evening routine, Miss Sinclair?" The camera man smiled as he watched the pretty blonde put on her overcoat.

"That is the plan, Randy." Her smile was brilliant as she placed a matching wool hat over her head. "Enjoy your dinner with Cindy and give her my love. See you at ten."

"Yes, and thanks, I'll give Cindy your message." He watched her walk from the studio then smiled over at the show's director. "You know Beth, I wish Victoria could meet a good fellow to fill her life. On the outside, she seems so happy, but she has to be lonely when she's not working."

"Randy, I am sure if God has that special fellow somewhere for our Vicky, he will see that they get together." Beth Riggins picked up her bag and slung it over her shoulder, then patted the camera man on his back. "I'm off! My husband Theo is waiting with my dinner and your Cindy called and needs you to pick up an extra-large pizza for the both of you, plus those two growing boys. Now scoot, see you at ten."

Victoria prepared the meal for two, steak, salad and roasted potatoes. Her boyfriend had promised to bring the wine, as usual. She really loved Eric, a college professor in the neighboring town of Charlotte. Eric had a great personally, was paid top salary and was extremely handsome, especially when he smiled.

They usually ate at her apartment, never in his that he rented to be near her and they rarely ever went out in public. Eric had said crowds bothered him, large or small, after being around hundreds of students five days a week. He had rather spend their moments together, alone.

Even though Eric had told Victoria how much he loved her, he would never bring up marriage. Her love for Eric was so strong, she never brought up marriage, in fear of jeopardizing their relationship, so Victoria would try and be content with their arrangement.

Eric was loyal to his career and spent evenings at home going over classwork and test results from his many students. So, their days had been sat for Tuesdays and Saturdays, from 7:30 until 9:30p.m. Only once, since they had been seeing each other, did they go out of town together for the weekend. Eric had his annual reunion with a secret men's club in Salem,

Mass. The meetings lasted only a couple hours each day, so it left quality time for her and Eric to spend doing things, much of it in the hotel room making love. To Victoria, it was her favorite memory.

She checked her reflection in the mirror. Eric would be arriving exactly at 7:30 sharp. A handsome smile on his face and a bottle of French wine in his hand. They would eat, make small talk, then as always, they would end up in bed, making passionate love.

The only time Eric would make excuses not to come was when Victoria had her monthly period. She kept telling herself he was not using her only for sex, even though deep down, she could not help but think that when she sat alone on those nights.

The doorbell chimed out as the mantle clock struck 7:30, Eric had arrived. As always, there was a warm kiss at the door, dinner by candlelight and a very romantic hour in bed before his final goodnight kiss at the door and the words "See you Tuesday, unless class work comes up." Yes, unless there was some extra preparation he "had" to get ready for class Wednesday morning.

Victoria checked her desk calendar as she prepared her final makeup before leaving for work and noticed a red circle around Monday, the time for her period. What excuse will Eric come up with this time, until he is free to come on Saturday. She looked at herself in the mirror and whispered

"When will I learn? I just love him so much." Victoria glanced down at the post card sent from the church she used to attend. She smiled at the picture of Mary and baby Jesus before turning it over to read.

"Come, join us as we celebrate the Holy Season and the coming of Christmas!" Victoria looked back at the cover and said softly "Can I find my answer there in that little white church, filled with loving, caring people?" she checked her watch. She had twenty minutes to make it to the station by ten.

If she were ten minutes late, no one there would judge her. Victoria worked beside of warm friendly people who felt more like family. They each were filled with that special kind of faith that made you feel good to be around. Such dear devoted Christians.

Beth, her boss and dear friend, Randy, who served as youth minister in his church and Carl, the weatherman, who's beautiful bass voice got him lots of solos in his church choir. Working next to such devoted church goers was the reason Victoria had never told them about Eric. Having sex out of wedlock might be frowned upon and they all respected and loved their news anchor.

All the worrying and wine had given Victoria a spitting headache, so she grabbed some pain tablets before leaving. That was when she spotted the round pill pack in the bottom of the drawer and her heart began to pound as fear overtook her. She grabbed the pack up and found it full. She had never opened them. Victoria had simply forgotten to take her birth control pills for the entire month of November.

She grabbed her mouth to snaffle her scream of shock as she, blurt out "God! I cannot be pregnant!" her shaky fingers found her desk chair and she fell in it. "Please no, no! Eric will hate it! He hates kids, said he never wanted any! Just me and him!"

Victoria sit there in a daze. She would be late, but she would be forgiven by her co-workers. Would Eric forgive her forgetfulness?

Chapter 4

"Regina, my child, must you go to that place tonight?" A worried father had dropped by with a few groceries for his twenty-five-year old daughter. "Why don't you stay home and make some of that nice vegetable soup like your mama used to fix?"

"Pop, sweet caring pop! It is only a job and it pays very well." She leaned over and kissed the five-foot-eight-inch older man, whose sadness shown clearly on his wrinkled face. "I must support me and Joby, not to mention what I am saving for nurse's school." Regina's six-inch heels made her tower above her frail, snooped over father.

"Have you been out to see Mama today?" looking in the hall mirror, Regina applied a rich red lipstick, checked her blonde hair and called up the stairs. "Joby, your grandpop is here. Get your things and come on down."

"Coming mama!" A soft young voice called down as the elderly man stood at the bottom of the steps gazing up. He recalled her question about visiting his Margaret so he said softly, "I took her some fresh flowers. The last ones got frozen." His old eyes remained on the steps, looking for his granddaughter to come down. "She still thinks you work as a waitress, Gina?"

"Of course, Papa. Joby is only six." Regina put her arm lovingly around his thin shoulders. "I'm going to have to make that vegetable soup for you soon Pop, with a big pan of cornbread, before you blow away with the wind." He smiled up at her and turned his attention back on the stairs. "Pop, why do you keep buying mama real flowers to put on her grave this time of year? Artificial ones are very pretty and reliable for the cold winter."

He turned to stare at her. "Artificial? Poppycock! My

beautiful Margaret Rose loved real flowers, and by cracky, if I have to replace them every day, I will!" Regina laughed softly and kissed the top of his white head.

"The flower shops will love you." Looking back up the stairs, Regina spotted her daughter coming down the steps, dressed in her favorite too-too and tights, covered by her favorite oversize sweater, one of her late daddy's.

"Young lady, I hope you got your warm p j's in that bag and something nice to wear for church tomorrow morning."

"I packed my flannel p j's and my red wool dress for church. I know Jesus loves to see pretty children." Joby hugged her grandfather around his neck when he stooped over to kiss her. "I love you, grandpop! My Sunday school teacher Miss Martha, told us we were Jesus' little lambs. I really love Jesus!"

"That I know, bright eyes! Jesus loves you an extra heap, and so does your old grandpop!" He took her small suitcase and nodded toward his daughter. "Give your mama a big kiss and hug."

"You be a good girl for your grandpop, kid-o and I will pick you up from school Monday afternoon." Regina kissed her dark-haired daughter and watched them drive away.

Saturday nights were busy at Sadie's Ladies and even though they lived in the small town of Maglen, gentlemen came from surrounding cities and towns for various reasons. To keep such business dealings private, to keep wives from getting suspicious and the fact that the choice of prostitutes was high class as well as beautiful. Regina's favorite nights were Wednesday and Sunday, when her favorite client came in. The way she felt about Eric, Regina would have almost give her services free to him, but she needed money for nursing school, after which she would retire from Sadie's and start a good descent career. One her pop would be proud of and better still, her Lord. Regina had felt she had let God down by becoming a prostitute, but it was something she was good

17

at and the men always ask for her. Maybe it was her wit and charm, they found irreplaceable, but more likely, it was Regina's well stocked breast, shapely hips, small waist and long blonde hair.

Her eyes fell on her calendar where she had circled her starting date. One more week with Eric before she had her period. It would appear for some reason, Eric made special trips on those days. It was the only time Regina didn't work and she called it, her client free week off. She spent those days doing fun things with Joby and her loving father.

Saturday came and went and Regina was too tired to fix her usual snack of cheese, fruit and a glass of merlot. She went straight to the shower no matter how late or tired she was, she had to shower off after having sex with three different men. It made her feel cheap, dirty and ashamed, at least until she reminded herself why she became a hooker in the first place.

The last thing Regina always made sure to do was to take out her morning after pills so she would remember to take them in the morning, following sex. She noticed there was only one pill left in the bottom of the bottle. Grabbing a pad and pen, she wrote herself a note to refill the prescription tomorrow before work.

Regina smiled to herself seeing Eric's handsome face in her mind. Eric was not work, but she still needed to take those pills. The last thing she needed was a baby and Regina did not know if she could go through another slip up and end up having another abortion. The nightmares had finally stopped haunting her since her last one. The plain cold facts were, Regina could not afford to get pregnant, both financially or mentally.

The next afternoon, Regina walked from the drug store with what she called her safe pills. Slipping the small bag inside her purse for safe keeping, she made her way to Sadie's Ladies Gentlemen Parlor. The beautiful blonde had spent extra time getting ready. She wanted to look her absolute best for her favorite customer. Eric always paid for the entire night because he wanted Regina all to himself and as usual, food arrived in her private quarters. Because Regina was a favorite of Sadie's rich customers, her rooms were furnished with the finest bed, table and chairs along with a plush love seat, expensive china, crystal wine glasses and stain glass Tiffany lamps. Sadie had placed the wine cabinet full with expensive wine, unless, like Eric, the client preferred bringing his own wine.

"Miss Regina, your gentleman friend ordered the most romantic dinner for you this evening." The owner of LaBella French Restaurant placed the warm covered plates in the oven and set the table with a crisp white tablecloth. Flowers, candles, silver wear and folded napkins completed the elegant table setting. He took the crystal wine glasses out of the glass cabinet and placed them carefully down, then stood back to admired his artistic work. His smile showed his approval as he turned to the beautiful women sitting gracefully on the love seat.

"Now Miss Regina, the wine bucket is being chilled in your refrigerator, along with two beautiful salads and a luscious authentic French cheesecake." He smiled knowingly and bowed his head politely. "Please enjoy your dinner and have a wonderful evening." With that, he walked from the room carrying his hot and cold bags.

Eric arrived right on time, a smile on his handsome face and an expensive bottle of French wine in his hand.

"Regina, you are the most beautiful woman I have ever had the pleasure in knowing." He set the bottle down and pulled her into his arms. "You know you are my special girl and there is no one else I had rather be with."

"As well as you know, you are my favorite fellow and I would be happy to be in your arms every night, my darling." Regina felt her usual butterflies when Eric's lips melted over hers.

As promised, the dinner was very romantic, the French wine excellent and after a small slice of the yummy cheesecake, Eric's bedroom eyes told Regina it was time to move to the bedroom. Eric was the perfect gentleman, making slow romantic moves, touching, kissing. But when he got into the actual act of love making, Eric could be demanding, take full control of the female body. Eric knew how to make a woman feel good, feel special, but he made sure his need was always met.

"I may be calling you on Tuesday next week beautiful, as well as our days." His hand moved slowly down her blonde hair.

"Then you will be free except of course Mondays, Thursdays and Fridays." Eric had told Regina those three days were set aside for his mother. She had respected him for that, knowing he cared for his widow mother was a warm blessing. "You know next Friday I have my week off." Regina could not bring herself to call it her period week, no sex, but Eric seem to read between the lines.

"Come to think of it, Regina, that was the week I promised to take mother on a little trip to visit her sister in Virginia." Eric kissed her goodnight and closed the door.

As Regina climbed from her shower, she looked through her closet and pulled out a short red dress.

"Eric liked this one on me. I will wear it Tuesday night." She smiled and crawled under the sheets. "At least I'll be with him for three nights before he leaves to spend time with his mother." She pulled the covers up and smiled. "He will really be ready for me when he returns from Virginia after a week without sex."

Despite having three days with Eric, the week flew by. Each night with Eric was special and their love making was hot and steamy. It was extra hard to pull away from one another on Saturday night and even Eric was surprised he got aroused again, so they remained in bed another hour longer than usual.

Breathing heavy from going twice, Eric checked his watch and frantically jumped out of bed and dressed quickly, his eyes wild with panic.

"Regina, I have got to go now! I cannot wait for you to get up! Just lie there and rest!" he leaned over and brushed her lips lightly with his, turned and raced out the door.

Regina straightened up her fancy rooms and looked inside her purse for her car keys.

"Darn keys, always falling to the bottom!" she dumped the contents on the messy bed and her eyes flew open. The small unopened pharmacy bag lay in the mess of items. "How stupid!" she thought "that I forgot my pills! Dear God, no!" Regina had not taken one morning after pill after having sex with Eric for three nights and with her period due Sunday, her eggs would really be ready for fertilization. Regina knew Eric was the only man she had sex with since she had marked out the other nights to save herself for Eric, the man she loved. Regina also knew she was easy to get pregnant, because Joby was conceived the first time she had sex.

It was different then. She was about to graduate from Maylen High School; and her heart belonged to one boy. Michael Joby Marshall.

Chapter 5

Regina and Michael had been sweethearts in high school ever since she became a freshman. Mike was a junior, athletic and the best-looking guy in old Maglen High. Michael Joby competed in almost all the sports the school offered and he excelled in basketball, football, and baseball. No game sport seemed out of his reach and he ranked first in each sport, bringing his school to victory after victory,

Although Michael loved sports, his greatest happiness was spending time with his girl, Regina. Everyone at school admired them as the most handsome couple on campus. Not just their obvious good looks but both of them had giving manners they showed each of their classmates. An all-round perfect couple, loved by staff and students.

When Mike got out of school, he had a job waiting for him at his father's company, Marshall's Sporting and Hardware Store. Being an only child, Michael would inherit the popular store one day and knowing sports, he loved helping customers in that department.

The plan was, as soon as Regina graduated, they would get married and she could start working as cashier in the family owned business. Regina and Mike had decided to wait a couple of years before starting a family, to save for their own home. For the time being, Regina and Mike lived in the family's guest home. A small one room cottage with a small kitchen and single bathroom. The loving couple did not mind the small space, they had each other and that was enough.

As was the family custom, the hardware store was always closed on Sunday, to give the owners and employees the Sabbath off, to rest and attend the church of their choice. Regina especially loved sitting next to Michael in church, just to listen to his beautiful baritone voice sing the old familiar hymns. She had expressed the need for him to sing in the choir. Even the choir director and many of the choir members, had approached him and invited him to join them. Deep inside, Regina was happy Mike chose to sit next to his wife.

Try as they might, Regina found herself pregnant and to top it off, she was already well into her pregnancy. Six months, the same length of time they had been married, so they both decided Regina had gotten pregnant on their honeymoon at Myrtle Beach, South Carolina.

Despite Regina worrying about the bad timing, Michael was overjoyed with the ideal of having a baby. He had told her "Sometime our plans are over road by God's plan for us. My darling Regina, this baby is a gift, as is every child the Lord blesses you with. A baby is so helpless and innocent, it is up to us, it's parents, to make sure it is always loved and feels safe. What a blessing to be the father, but you, my darling Regina, you are the mother and God has blessed you with the special job of feeling our baby grow. Our Lord God has given us this precious gift to take care of and he or she is a part of you and a part of me, and that makes our baby, a part of our love."

Regina was totally happy. She had Michael's undying love and a baby on the way, but her joy was short lived. The doctor told her and Mike there could be complications with the baby, and there was a 90% chance it could be deformed. Regina had wept in Michael's strong arms as he tried to comfort her with his soft loving words.

"Regina, there are times when God hands out little babies that are not completely perfect in man's eyes, but our Heavenly Father loves that tiny soul no less than he does the heathiest baby born. I think God gives those special children to those of us who love with our heart, not our eyes. That little baby will be so precious and small, it will need all the love we can give it. The baby never asked to be put there, but our love planted the seed and God Place the soul he had chosen for this wee one. You need not be sad, my darling, our loving Lord will help us, one day at a time."

"Regina" she could still see Michael's tear-filled eyes and the beautiful glow about him. "I will love our baby the same as I did when we found out about..." she remembered how Mike had hesitated for a moment, as though he could hear someone speaking to him, then he said softly, "about her. She will always be daddy's little girl."

Tears fell down Regina's cheeks as she looked down at the photograph in her trembling hands. She had often wondered how Michael had known their unborn baby would be a girl. It was still a beautiful mystery. Then there was the glow that appeared around his handsome face. Was it the light of Jesus, our Savior, reflecting on him, knowing he would be going home to heaven in a few short hours from that moment?

Regina clutched the photo to her chest as she remembered back to that last kiss before Michael left the cottage to go opened the store for his sick father.

"My wonderful, caring Michael. You could have stood back and watched like the other frighten witnesses on the street. But your loving heart and Christ-like call, to lay down your life for others, drove you into action."

Those watching on the streets had told Regina later, they heard Michael whisper before dashing across the street, "My love Regina, God calls. If I do not return, I will wait for you in Heaven. Our little girl, our little Joby, will be healthy, thank you Jesus! She will be a constant reminder of me and our love, my dearest darling. Always know, I love you!"

With that, Michael ran to save two little children clinging on a tree limb above a fallen live electric wire. As he ran, he pulled two strong men with him and ordered them to stand a short distance away so he could throw each man one of the frighten children. Michael knew the tree limb would not support the weight of him and the children for a very long length of time, so he had to act fast. The limb hung down away from any safe branch, so the only way to save those innocent kids was to crawl out on the same limb. The odds were slim that he would survive but Michael knew the small frighten children had only begun their lives and he knew he had known the greatest love known to man. Wonderful parents, great friends, his Regina, the love of his life and heart, and a beautiful Savior, who had shown Michael how much He loved him by laying down His life for all.

If he lived, Michael thought, it would be a blessing to grow old with Regina. If he died, he would live again in peace and glory forever. That faithful day, Michael Joby Marshall went to live with Jesus after throwing two small children in one of his greatest pitches ever, and his last on earth.

"Oh Mike, you would be so proud of Joby. She is so much like you, my darling. So athletic! She's on her softball team as the pitcher and she can really throw a real stinger, as you used to call your throws. She is also on her basketball team! Can you believe that? Just, six-years-old and ringing the net every throw!" Regina smiled, seeing her little girl excelling at sports just like her daddy. "Your daughter has even tried out for the boy's pee football team and after seeing her throws and catches, the team is considering accepting her as the first girl ever to play. Like I said, just like her daddy." Her attention fell on her daughter in her tights and ballet costume. She picked up the picture and laughed. "There is still a little bit of me in our baby girl, Mike. She loves to dress up and dance. Her beautiful eyes and dark black hair she got from you." Regina picked up the full pill bottle, still sealed and looked at the picture of her and Michael on the wall. "Mike, I have made a mess of my life. If only you were still alive, my dearest."

Then she remembered getting pregnant the second time because of one stupid missing pill. She recalled getting up early to start her morning routine. Start the coffee pot, switch on the radio for the morning news and weather, then take her morning after pill. She had totally forgotten about Joby being out of school for a teacher's workday. Her father had picked her up from school the day before and stayed with her until he heard Regina drive in. Being tired and wanting a hot bath, Regina barely remembered why her father couldn't watch her until later the following day. A doctor's appointment or something.

As Regina was about to take her last pill in the bottle, when Joby came running through the kitchen chasing their family dog and knocked the pill out of her mother's hand. Little Joby had just turned three and she stood frozen as she watched her mama crawling around on the kitchen floor, looking for the "safe" pill. It had simply vanished. When Regina went in the next morning to get a renewal for her medicine, her doctor refused because she was pregnant.

After talking it over with Sadie, a warm and kind woman, who, despite her business, genuinely cared about her girls, she convinced Regina to have an abortion as soon as possible, before the baby started growing. Sadie paid all the doctor's bills so Regina would not lose any of her hard earn savings.

Right after the abortion, Regina started having the dreams that haunted her night after night. Michael would appear in the dreams and they felt so real she could swear he was really there, speaking to her.

"Regina, there are times when God hands out little babies that are not completely perfect in man's eyes, but our heavenly Father loves that tiny soul. I think God gives that special baby to those of us who love with our heart and not our eyes. That baby never asked to be put there, but the seed has been sown and God has placed the soul He had chosen for this wee one. Regina, that little baby will be so precious and small, it will need all the love you can give it."

"Would she have done something different if the dreams had come before the abortion?" Regina thought, then spoke aloud "I can never go back and undo what I did and I just pray I am not faced with that same decision." She sat thinking, some three years later.

After making a visit to her doctor, Regina found herself in the same trouble, the doctor had confirmed it. She was expecting a baby. Now, how would Eric take the revelation? She had told him about her daughter, Joby, when he asked her if she had any children. Regina shared her story about her and Michael, their great love for one another, their beautiful daughter and his tragic death. Eric had assured her how much he loved children and hoped to meet her little girl someday. It appeared, little girls held a special place in Eric's heart and he wanted so much to make her a part of his life in the future.

Perhaps Eric will be happy about the baby, even ask her to marry him and live happily ever after, or did that only happen in fairy tales? Nevertheless, Regina knew she only had a short window before she made the decision.

Chapter 6

Eric Shields turned his Mercedes-Benz quickly down his long driveway. He could not control his sexual desires for Regina and it threw him off schedule. Being a constant planner and always on time, Eric shuttered at the thought of being late. This had been the second time and far too close the last time.

Eric was happy his big house set back off the main road, so the nosy neighbors couldn't see him come and go. He raced inside and up to his room, where he insisted to his devoted wife, Janet, that it only made sense to have separate bedrooms with ten in the big house and just the two of them. He looked at himself in the mirror, then climbed inside the hot shower, to wash away any evidence. The smell of perfume, a lady's make-up, sex smells and the luscious female cream on his privates.

"Dear Janet gets her share of sex from me, so she should count herself lucky." Eric laughed softly as he threw his clothes into a laundry bag. For his convenience, he sent his laundry out, informing his trusting wife it was one less thing for her to do on her busy schedule.

He checked his watch. He had finished just in time as he made his way down the wide staircase. Eric grabbed two wine glasses, a bottle of expensive merlot, then switched on his favorite music, opera. He looked up and smiled when he heard her car pull inside their three-car garage. Taking a sip, he closed his eyes and vision her expensive B.M.W. pulling to a stop at the far side, next to his Jaguar. His thoughts briefly went on Rebecca, then he brushed them aside until later, when he went up to bed for the night.

"How was your work tonight, darling? Hopefully no really sick patients." Eric kissed her as she stooped down wearily and brushed the wine away smiling, then fell into her comfortable chair and put her feet up.

"Working the evening shift has its awards, Eric. The nurses are very professional and highly trained for whatever shows up in E.R." Doctor Janet Shields got her degree at Harvard and she was top in her class. An excellent heart surgeon as well as a caring M.D. whenever she worked in the emergency room or wherever she was needed at Maglen General Hospital. Her staff loved her and she had respect for each of them. Janet spent her slow times in the hospital chapel, praying for her sick patients.

Being married to an unbeliever was hard, difficult at best, but Janet was madly in love with Eric and had been ever since she met him at Harvard, while he was visiting friends there. They had gotten married right after she got her doctor's degree and moved to the small town of Maglen, in the state of North Carolina. Janet had made the move for Eric who had landed a job teaching history at the local college. Duke tried to get her to join them, but she loved Eric and she could find a good hospital anywhere.

"I went by the gynecologist today before my shift." Janet observed Eric's behavior. He just smiled and closed his eyes.

"What did he say?"

"The baby is growing like a weed." She laughed softly. "I just love southern doctors. They can say the cutest things."

"Sound a bit red neck to me." Eric grunted, he did not like another man touching what belonged to him. He forced a smile. "So, this man could tell just by feeling your stomach the baby is growing? How far long are you, Janet?"

"Six months darling, and the doctor does not just feel to know how a baby is growing." Janet sat up, her eyes beaming. "I saw the baby today! Oh Eric, he is so tiny. I wish you could come with me next time to see your son."

"I wish that too dearest, but you know I cannot miss classes." Eric picked up a folder filled with the theme papers. "All these papers have been marked. Most of the students got a B grade. One student got an A+." he laughed sarcastically.

"And her theme paper was not even on a real person in history, at least not who she said he was and her facts were mere fiction. But it was well written so I had to award her the A+."

"What was her theme about, Eric?" Janet kicked off her shoes and laid her head back, knowing she would just have to put them right back on before going up to bed. She wished it were already Thursday night so she could have her Friday evening with Eric.

"Her foolish theme paper was on Jesus, titled: 'He Walked in Galilee". It was very amusing to think one so young and talented could be brain wash into thinking this Jesus was the Son of God. A God who does not exist."

"She sounds like a lovely person." Janet slipped her feet inside her white shoes and stood up, stretching. "I'm off to bed. See you in the morning."

"Janet, there is really no need for you to get up early every morning to have coffee with me and see that I get off." Eric got up to walk with her to their separate bedrooms. He laid the folder down on the hall side table before climbing the stairs. Janet took his arm and laid her head over on his shoulder.

"I enjoy our mornings Eric. Besides, these short few minutes we have at night is our only time together, other than our Friday evenings, which I always look forward to."

"I enjoy our time together as well, Janet. Making love to my beautiful wife is always an enjoyable event." He kissed her when they reached the bedroom doors. "You know I would make love to you more often if you weren't so exhausted after working so long." Eric pulled her into his arms and kissed her passionately. "I love you doc. Sweet dreams."

"I love you too, teacher." She smiled "Dream about me, my love. Good night." She slipped inside her room as Eric smiled to himself.

"I'll dream about you later, when that baby is out of my girl's belly." He walked inside his dark room and dropped his pajamas on the floor and climbed into bed naked. "Rebecca, to feel your breast again and that moment I took her virginity." His hand moved down to his hard on as he closed his eyes and visualized making love to his young student.

As always, Janet got down to the kitchen first to start the coffee. As she passed the hall table, she noticed Eric's folder which contained his student's theme papers. She picked them up and glanced through them for "He Walked in Galilee" by Rebecca Bradford. Luckily it lay near the top of the stack and right under it was one titled: "To Have Lived and Loved Casanova" by Deanne Fuller. Janet laughed softly as she slipped it under the Bradford girl's top-grade A+ report, pretty rare grade for Eric to hand out. She looked at the A+ marked across the top of the paper in red ink and mumbled.

"Eric must have been impressed! Too bad it did not touch his heart and make him a believer. But that would take, a walk-on-water miracle."

Knowing Eric always came down just in time for a quick cup of coffee before going off to the job he loved, Janet knew she had time to read both theme papers before he appeared, looking like he had just stepped out of a male model magazine. Eric never minded her reading them. He respected her opinion on his grading and judgment and he knew she always agreed with his decisions. Miss Bradford deserved the A+ rewarded. It was obvious to, Janet, the young lady knew her Bible well. Her detail remarks had been stunning and Janet found her heart leaping with total joy and love when she finished reading it.

Miss Fuller's theme paper was somewhat cheesy and a bit off the wall. It seemed to be more of a young girl's fantasy than a report on the actual events and places in the life of the great Casanova, lover to women.

Janet was laughing softly to herself when Eric made his entrance, looking dashing as always. She watched her husband as he poured his coffee and thought "Students like Miss Fuller might see Eric as a romantic figure, from his good looks, at least in a young women's imagination. Could these words she had written really been about her and Eric? In the mind of a flirty student only." Janet smiled at her handsome husband as he sat down next to her. "I know I can trust him." She thought as she watched him pick up the two, theme papers and stack them neatly before taking his first sip. "Eric is very devoted to me and our marriage."

"It's a delight to hear you laugh so early in the morning, my dear. One of these papers seem to bring out your sense of humor. Was it the fiction?"

"Actually, it was the fiction, Eric. The paper titled: "To Have Lived and Loved Casanova". I found it very amusing, to say the least and I would consider it a comedy. There's not much truth there, but it's pretty entertaining. I'm not sure it deserves an A though, darling." Janet reached for the morning paper to read later. She had a long morning alone and plenty of time to read the news. Eric forced a smile down at her.

"I'm sorry you disagree with my judgement Janet, but I found Miss Fuller's paper very interesting."

"I suppose most men would like it. There is quite a bit of sex in to for a college freshman's paper. You might even describe it as trashy, as though the girl is sending out hints of flirting or maybe an open invitation." Janet rose to get the coffee pot, then filled her cup and offered her husband some more. He smiled and waved it away.

"I've got to be heading out in a few minutes. I'll grab another cup in the faculty lounge before heading to my classroom." He stood up and slid the stack of theme papers back inside the folder. "How did you like Miss Bradford's topic?"

"I found it completely beautiful and actuate. She deserves the A+, darling. There, I agree with you 100%." Janet gave him a real smile.

"That's good, I'm glad we agree on one." Eric bent down and kissed her. "Miss Bradford's ability to write fiction is a rewarding gift."

Chapter 7

Professor Shields had made it a point to walk down the hall pass the music department. As always, his timing was perfect. He could hear Rebecca Bradford going over her vocals. He smiled to himself and whispered

"The voice of an angel." He turned and continued down the long hallway to his classroom, A big bronze plaque over the door read, Eric Shields, Professor of History. When he stepped inside, he noticed Deanne Fuller was already sitting in her front row seat, a few minutes ahead of schedule. Her long brown ponytail swung around as she turned to watch the handsome teacher walk in and go behind his desk. Her voice held a hint of flirting when she spoke up.

"Good morning Professor Shields. That is a smart shirt you're wearing today. The color looks real nice on you."

"Thank you, Miss Fuller. I take it your last class let out early." Eric looked over his glasses as he pulled books and papers out of his briefcase and placed them neatly on his large desk in the middle of the large classroom. "Do you always wear your hair in that ponytail, Miss Fuller?"

"You may call me Deanne, if you like. It's much friendlier." She smiled "If I could, I would call you Eric."

"Why not Casanova? I caught your drop meaning in your theme paper, hints you were referring to me." Eric looked up at the clock when she glanced down, embarrassed. "I am truly flattered that a young- women would find me so appealing, but I grant you, Miss Fuller, I am nothing like Casanova. I am a happily married man and very devoted to my wife."

"I never meant anything would become of what I wrote, sir." Deanne smiled up at the handsome man. "and although you might not be aware of it, you are 'very' hot!"

Eric laughed softly as some of the other students began

filing into his class. The 'hot' conversation came to a halt as the room filled, Rebecca and her cousin Brook, were among the last to arrive.

"Class, I was very pleased and somewhat amused at some of your theme papers you turned in on Saturday. Your choices of subjects, times and places in history all varied. Most of you chose a person written in history with two exceptions, Kyle Berrier had a remarkable piece on Secretariat, the racehorse and Nicci Perry's paper, was priceless. She chose Mickey Mouse, different but with great imagination. Both Kyle and Nicci got a B+.

The top three papers got A-, A, and the top paper got an A+. They were, Brook Falls, an A- on Mark Twain," Professor Shields walked back to Brook's seat and placed his hand on her shoulder as the shy young girl glanced down at her hands resting on her lap. "Many of you might not know this about this very shy girl, but Brook is the youngest of three children, all named after a body of water. Besides Brook, there is her sister, Spring, and her brother, River. It would appear her mother's name is Sea and her father's name is Wade Falls. It takes a big imagination to think of this family of water, but this is my take. The father wades in the brook, the spring, and the river till he falls over the sea."

The class began laughing at the funny scene put before them, seeing a man stepping in a brook, then a spring, then a river until he reached the sea, where he falls over it. But Rebecca could see the real meaning behind Eric Shields rude remark. The father wades sexually in Brook, Spring, then River before he falls on Sea, his wife." Rebecca looked down quickly when his eyes caught her watching him and a knowing smile crept across his lips.

"Some of you could make a double meaning out of my remark, right Rebecca?" she looked up to see his eyes still held hers.

"I assure you, Professor Shields, I do not know what you

are referring to." This time Rebecca did not look away. "Who got the A grade, sir?"

"The A theme paper went to Deanne Fuller, for her rousing rendition on the life and loves of Casanova." He smiled to himself as he picked up the last theme paper winner. "I must say the student who received the A+, gave a convincing write up, He Walked in Galilee. She is correct about a person name Jesus, who lived two thousand years ago, but as you read, one can tell where reality ends and fantasy began. Like most people who believe this nonsense, Rebecca Bradford has strong convictions in her beliefs. These beliefs have been planted inside her since she was old enough to understand things she was told.

Nevertheless, it is well written, a top nosh fiction, filled with magic and entertainment." He looked Rebecca in the eyes. "Would you care to comment, Miss Bradford?"

"Professor Shields, my faith teaches me to turn the other cheek. There are many kinds of strikes, sir. Some are physical." Her eyes burned on him. "Then there are the kind you just gave me, mere words, but words that are meant to hurt me and put down my belief in my Savior. Sir, there is no amount of words you can say that would alter my faith in God. All your great knowledge of history and its facts, cannot hold a candle to the knowledge that one book, the Holy Bible, has contained within its bindings. From start to finish, God's word is true and there is no one or nothing that can change it! Man, and man's word can and will die away, vanish from the earth! Even the earth itself, will vanish, but God's word can never die! It is Eternal!"

Professor Shields slowly clapped his hands as a sneer fell on his lips. "Nice speech! They certainly have made a believer out of you, Miss Bradford. Due to the fact that your theme did get the highest grade, despite being totally made up, I will let you slide by, this time, with your pitiful sermon."

"Forgive me sir, but Rebecca was speaking the truth."

Brook's voice shook from the looks she was receiving from her professor. In her heart, Brook knew she had to speak up for Jesus despite making Mr. Shields angry at her.

"Nothing more from you, young lady!" Eric squeezed her shoulder then looked around at the rest of the class observing him. "That goes for the rest of you students who feels the need to defend Rebecca or this Jesus!" he walked angrily behind his desk and slammed down the theme paper. "For your homework, I want you to read about any president in history and be prepared to discuss him next class! Dismissed!"

As the students were leaving, Eric stepped in front of Rebecca, her cousin Brook stopped to wait for her at the door and to listen to what he had to say.

"From now on, Miss Bradford, keep your religion to yourself!" he set his jaw. "Remember, this is my class and I am the history teacher! You are here to learn from me, not the other way around! Do I make myself clear, Miss Bradford?"

Rebecca looked into his unblinking eyes as she thought, how easily it could have been Eric Shields who raped her. Her voice came out slow and sure "I understand Professor Shields, and I heard…'everything' you have said!" Rebecca thought she noticed a slight change, an uncertain look in those dark eyes, before he moved out of her way.

"Just do as I say! Next time, I won't be so gentle on you!" he turned and walked back to his desk as Rebecca fled the room and left quickly with her cousin.

Deanne Fuller had hung behind, gathering her books slowly as she listened to their conversation. She made her way slowly to the door, then turn to look back at her handsome Professor.

"Professor Shields, you can't let Rebecca Bradford bother you, sir. She has been a church nut ever since elementary school and there is nothing that will change her mind." She laughed softly. "I would not be surprised if the goodie good became a nun."

"Then that would be a pity, robbing some young man the honor of marring such a beautiful young lady." Eric took in the young body standing close to him. "Tell me Deanna, have you ever considered going blonde?"

"Blonde? My hair?" she reached up laughing and bounced her ponytail, then looked up seriously into Eric's eyes. "Would you like that, Mr. Shields?"

"Well, it's really not for me to say, but…" he stood up and walked to her, then removed the hair band from her ponytail, then brushed through her hair with his hands, causing it to fall over her shoulders. "That's better." Deanna felt her heart racing from his touch. His voice came out slow and seductive "Yes, blonde would suit your pretty face."

Deanna reached up and took his hand that was resting on her cheek. "Eric?"

"Better run along now. You'll be late for your next class." Eric knew he had turned on the young naive girl. "I will see you Monday morning."

"Al…alright." She backed up, eyes dreamy and her face flushed, then she turned and quickly raced from the room.

Chapter 8

"Mama, can I ask you a personal question?" Rebecca knew she must cross out her own father as the rapist, so she could narrow her list of suspects.

"What's on your mind, Rebecca?" her mother took her hands, seeing the anxious look on her daughter's face. "I know there has been something bothering you ever since your father and I returned from the sale. Your coldness toward your daddy was troubling and it has upset him greatly."

"Was it that obvious?" Rebecca had tried to act normal when her parents arrived home on Monday morning before classes began. She had tried to make excuses for not hanging around to greet them properly when they got home. Even the times she was at home, she kept her distance from the man she had always loved and respected.

"Tell me child, what is bothering you?"

"Mama, at the sale, was daddy with you the entire time you were there? Was he there on Friday night?" Rebecca bit her fingernails nervously, something she had not done for a very long time. Her mother took her hand down from her mouth and held it in hers.

"Friday night? It's funny you should ask about Friday night, baby." She thought back. "We got in late that afternoon. The sale had gone on later that evening, so we decided to order out, only no place open had delivery." Rebecca's mother watched her daughter carefully as she continued. "I decided to remain at the motel and have a much need bath while your father went out to get our take-out. He was a little late returning, said there had been some sort of a wreck ahead of him on the highway. He found out as he got closer that some poor farmer's hay had slid off his wagon onto the road, causing the road to be shut down until the hay was cleared away."

"How long was the delay, mama?" Rebecca tried to keep her voice calm, but she knew she still sounded anxious.

"Rebecca, what on earth happened to you?"

"Please mama, just tell me. Did daddy have time to drive home, stay at least one hour, then drive back?" Rebecca knew her words were confusing to her mother, but she had to be sure.

"Good Lord, Rebecca! There was absolutely no way for John to drive the four hours home, stay one hour, then drive four hours back! That is nine hours!" Mrs. Bradford pulled her daughter over to the sofa. "I do not know what you are keeping from us, Rebecca, but I can assure you, your daddy had no part in it. He came walking back into our room about one hour and twenty minutes after he left, with our food."

"My heart knew daddy would not do it, but the one that did, knew words daddy had spoke to me, here, in our home." Rebecca knew she had to break the bad news to her mother so, she took a big breath. "The intruder set other men up as well, throwing me off his own scent."

"Intruder? In our home? Alone with you child?" Mary Bradford was suddenly troubled. "And this man had the nerve to set up your own father? What kind of animal could do such a thing?"

"The same kind of animal who could rape a helpless girl, mama." Tears streamed down Rebecca's face as her mother's face reflected her own. "Yes mama, this evil man raped me in my bedroom, where he was hiding and waiting."

"No wonder you were afraid to get near poor John." Mary Bradford hugged her daughter tightly. "Who else is on your list of suspects? Maybe we can narrow them down to the rapist."

"Ned Shoemake, the pharmacist at Maglen Drug Store, Tony Spangler..." Rebecca's mother gasp.

"Anthony Spangler? The church choir director?"

"It gets even worse mama, Reverend Anderson." She took

her mother's shaking hands. "I know it hard to imagine either of those two church leaders as a rapist, but he knew words they had spoken to me, at church and usually when no one else was around."

"Rebecca, I cannot believe that Preston would do anything as vile as raping an innocent member of his church. I realize Priest have been caught doing these un-godly things, but Preston is very devoted to Terresa and his three sons are the apple of his eye."

"The last two suspects are Buck and my history professor, Mr. Shields. It would be very easy for me to point my finger at Professor Shields, but I cannot be certain and the Lord has told us to never judge another person." Rebecca laid her head back on the sofa and waited for her mother to regain her senses before telling her more. Mary's face was white as she rung her hands nervously.

"I'm afraid Buck does look somewhat suspicious, darling. As you know, Buck went with us to Rock Creek for the sale. John holds Buck's opinions to a high standard and thinks he knows all there is to know about raising cows for breeding and resale."

"Why do you suspect Buck, mama? Did he leave Rock Creek?" Rebecca was hoping it could not be Buck Fowler, her father's right-hand man for six years. Buck didn't have any family left, at least none the family knew about. Her parents had fixed up the guest cottage into an apartment for the handy man. He rarely went to town on his spare time and didn't seem to have many friends. He seemed content to hang around the farm, maybe go fishing at the big pond. Buck was considered, by the family almost a family member. He was kind, easy going, somewhat shy and backward. Perhaps the results of having quit school at fifteen. Rebecca was only twelve when he came by looking for a job and her daddy took him in. She just did not want to believe it was this friendly man that always had a warm smile or a kind word. Rebecca looked up when she heard her mother speak.

"Buck came to John on Friday morning and said he needed to go back to Maglen. He told John, Weber's Bank had sent him word that he needed to come into the bank sometime before closing time on Friday, to sign a loan contract for his new pickup truck." Mary stood up and walked to the window. Trying to spot the handy man outside. "I haven't seen any new truck parked out at the cottage." Mary turned to look at her daughter who was taking in her words. "When he was speaking to your father in Rock Creek, Buck seemed a bit nervous, but we thought it was because we would not be there to help him read over the bank loan contract. Bucks reading skills are poor to bad. I remember he promised John he would leave extra early on Saturday morning to get back for the big sale at ten."

"Buck would have had time to get to the house and wait for me in my bedroom. He also knew where the spare key to the house is kept." Rebecca joined her mother at the window. "That brings up another clue. The rapist knew the layout of our house and which room was mine. When I was downstairs, I heard a creak on the upstairs floor, two different times. I thought it was the pine floors adjusting to the changing temperatures, then I heard it a third time..." a cold chill ran down her neck. "when the floor creaked directly behind me. Then I felt his hand touch my shoulder."

Mary turned and pulled Rebecca back into her arms, making her feel protected and loved. "Poor baby, you must have been frightened out of your mind."

"No one can really know just how frightening it can be, mama, unless it ever happened to them." Rebecca caught movement below the window. "Buck! He just came out of the woodshed carrying an ax."

"I heard John ask him to chop a load of wood from the wood pile beside the smoke house. Cold weather means lots of fires burning." Mary turned back to her daughter, a thought filling her mind. "I know how we can eliminate the possibility of his guilt, once and for all. I will pay the Weber Bank a visit and I know just the right approach to make."

"May I come with you mama? This thing has gotten even more serious." Rebecca knew it was time to lay out the bomb shell. "Mama, I think I'm pregnant!"

"God! You are pregnant by…only God knows who!" Mary blurted out. "Rebecca, are you absolutely certain, darling?"

"My period was due on Monday and I have never gone over a week mama. To top things, I feel nauseated most mornings and the thought of breakfast makes me sicker."

"I will call doctor Fuller and set you up an appointment, first thing Monday morning. You can take a sick day, it wouldn't be lying." Mary Bradford started for her desk when Rebecca grabbed her arm.

"Mama, I would rather go to a doctor who does not know me." Rebecca searched her mother's eyes for understanding. "Deanne is Doctor Fuller's daughter! She is in my history class and is always flirting with Professor Shields. She could find out and start telling everyone, including my top suspect."

"Darling, you know a doctor must not discuss his patient's health records with anyone." Mary patted her daughter on the arm "I'm sure we can trust our family doctor."

"Mama, families sit around the dinner table telling each other about their day's events. The good doctor knows I am in Deanne's class and that we have been going to school together ever since the first grade. He will tell his precious spoiled daughter everything and she will spread the gossip all over campus!" Rebecca put her foot down. "No mother! I will not go to Doctor Fuller! Find me a lady doctor. I know I would feel more relaxed around a woman when she starts asking questions."

"A, lady doctor? Of course, Doctor Janet Shields, one of the best in the country, not to mention, the best in the town of Maglen. The newspaper reported, 'We are lucky to have a doctor as dedicated and highly skilled as Doctor Janet Shields. A graduate of both Harvard and Duke University. She has got more degrees than a prestigious dog breeder." Mary winked at her daughter. "A bit of light humor from Mr. Willard of the Maglen Journal but after seeing an interview on the night news with Doctor Shields, I found her second to none. The respect and love she shows each individual patient is heart- warming." Mary started flipping through the yellow pages. "She works long hours as Maglen General Hospital and has a private practice on Fifth and Vine, where she sees patients three mornings a week. I hope she can work you in, darling."

"Mama, Professor Shields could be related to Doctor Shields! Suppose they're marriage?" Rebecca stood nervously looking over her mother's shoulder. "If she is his wife, her views on faith could be the same as his."

"And what are his views?" Mrs. Bradford glanced up at her daughter.

"Professor Shields is an atheist mama. He thinks our beliefs in God and Jesus are fiction and he, enjoys throwing his views in my face."

"If Doctor Shields is marriage to that lost soul, I can testify that she is right the opposite, Rebecca. Janet Shields was our guest speaker at the Methodist woman's annual ham supper two years ago and she is a devoted Christian and a strong woman of faith. The testimony she gave that night was heartwarming and compelling. It is hard to imagine someone like her being married to a non-believer."

"They say that opposites, attracts, but the Bible even speaks about our relations with a non-believer." Rebecca looked down at the open yellow pages and pointed out Doctor Janet Shield's number. "Make the appointment if she has an opening. I will go."

Chapter 9

"We are here to see Doctor Shields, Rebecca Bradford." Mary Bradford smiled down at the friendly receptionist. The receptionist handed the shy girl a clip board with paper attached.

"Please fill out the papers Miss Bradford and take them back with you when you are called."

As Rebecca filled out the many questions regarding all her personal heath history, she glanced over and whispered to her mother.

"I'm glad the bank confirmed Buck's story about having to sign that loan contract that Friday before they closed."

"And I'm even more glad Maggie Fisher heard us wondering where he went after leaving the bank." Mary spoke softly as she looked around at the other patients waiting to be seen. "I never dreamed our Buck was sweet on a woman."

"Buck keeps his private life to himself." Rebecca laughed softly, trying to imagine the shy handyman dating. "According to Miss Fisher, her and 'Buster' have been seeing each other for quite a while. I think this was the first time Buck slept with his girlfriend." The doctor's assistant broke through their conversation.

"Miss Bradford, the doctor will see you now." She noticed both women rose out of their chairs at the same time. Looking down at the anxious mother, the assistant nodded. "You may come back as well Mrs. Bradford, if you like."

"I certainly do wish to come and hear what Doctor Shields has to say to my daughter." When Mary Bradford made the appointment, she told the nurse on the phone she thought her daughter might be pregnant and they needed an appointment to see. Doctor Janet Shields read over the chart then walked inside and sat down.

"So, Rebecca, you think you're pregnant?" Janet remembered her name from the theme paper on Jesus as she measured up the nervous girl. "You also expressed the possibility of an abortion." She had read it from the chart Rebecca had just filled out. "Tell me Rebecca, did you use any form of birth control when you had sex?"

"Doctor Shields, my daughter had no reason to be on birth control! She is not sexually active!" Mary held tight to her daughter's trembling hand. "Rebecca is a good child and a strong young Christian."

"Mrs. Bradford, we choose to believe the best from our children, especially our young daughters." Janet hated to sound cold but she needed to find out what Rebecca was hiding. She knew from the theme paper that this girl's faith was real. As she waited for the mother to respond, Rebecca cried out

"I was raped!"

"Forgive me child, but I needed to know." Doctor Shields reached over and gently touched Rebecca's cheek. "Most rape victims are afraid to speak out, even if they know the creep who raped them."

"That's just the problem Doctor Shields, that animal was smart and clever to cover his tracks. Somehow, he knew personal conversations I had with a select group of men I'm acquainted with." For some reason, Rebecca felt like she could trust this woman with her secret. "He quoted remarks from six different men I came in contact with."

"Perhaps he had been stalking you for some time. Watching your routine or he could even have an inside source, feeding him with the things he knows about you." Rebecca admired Janet Shields' detective skills. "The man could have even set up six innocent men and not have referred to himself at all."

"I never thought of that possibility." She wiped her eyes dry as tears had started to flow, just talking about the rapist. "I'm so mixed up, Doctor Shields, I don't know what to do if

I am pregnant. I've just started college and I have my whole life ahead of me."

"Sweetheart." Mary Bradford touched her arm loving. "Whatever you decide, your daddy and I will stand behind you all the way."

"Thanks mama." Rebecca gave her a weak smile, torn between having an abortion or having this rapist's child.

"Rebecca, I may be able to help you, but before I mention my friend, I must ask, have you spoken to your minister?" Janet never rushed her patients in and out, she genuinely cared about people.

"I cannot go to Reverend Anderson. He is one of my suspects." Rebecca knew if this sweet caring woman ask her who the other men were, she would have to tell her.

"This person who raped you was heartless, Rebecca. Can you share the other five names? It's up to you dear. I'll not force you. You've had enough trauma in your life." Janet Shields held tight to the clip board, knowing how hard this must be for this sweet religious young woman.

"I'll tell you, I don't mind." Rebecca looked at her mother for approval and she nodded yes. "Tony Spangler, my choir director at church, Ned Shoemake, a pharmacist at Maglen Drug Store, our handy man, Buck Fowler, who has been cleared, my own father, also cleared and last of all...My history professor, Eric Shields."

"Eric?" Janet looked surprised for a moment, then laughed softly. "Excuse me Rebecca, but you can rule out Eric Shields. He is a very devoted husband who is usually so tired from teaching, he limits his love making with his understanding wife to one night a week." The doctor smiled beautifully and her innocents radiated over her pretty face. "Eric Shields is my husband, my dear. Don't let his stiff appearance and serious looks disturb you. He really is harmless."

"So, you know where your husband is when you are at work, on your late-night shifts?" Rebecca still did not trust her professor. She had witness firsthand, his flirty passes to the young women in her class, especially the ones with blonde hair.

"Rebecca, you must not make Doctor Shields distrust her husband, sweetheart." Mary Bradford looked embarrassed from her daughter's outburst.

"That's quite alright, Mrs. Bradford. I don't know what Eric does on those evenings. I just trust him." Janet could not understand the nagging feeling in the pit of her stomach. Was she second guessing her own belief in her 'devoted' husband.

"Let me narrow that down for you doctor. What about Friday evenings, do you know what he does on those evenings?" Rebecca could never forget that frightening Friday."

"That one is easy, my dear. I am off on Fridays, so Eric and I spend the entire evening together." Janet smiled, feeling relaxed.

"I see. Then you are off every Friday, Doctor Shields." Mary suddenly got drawn into the conversation. "What about the Friday, two weeks ago? That was the Friday night my daughter was raped?"

"I have a very big workload, Mrs. Bradford. There have been occasions when I'm called into work, due to an emergency heart operation or to replace a sick doctor on call. I will have to look back and check my calendar. My life is so busy, the weeks run into each other, but I'm sure I was off." Why was she covering for Eric if she trusted him so much, she wondered, clearly remembering the emergency surgery she had to perform two Friday evening ago.

"I'm truly sorry if I made you feel like I was pointing my finger at your husband, Doctor Shields." Rebecca had tears in her eyes "It's just so hard and I don't want to make the wrong decision and ruin my life forever."

"I know you have other patients waiting, Doctor Shields." Mary stood up and placed a loving hand on her daughter's shoulder. "You said you could help Rebecca if she is pregnant, make the right decision."

"Of course. My friend, Father Zechariah Benjamin will return to Maglen in a week and I can assure you, Rebecca, if anyone can help you with this problem, he can. It is his passion, his soul purpose in life to help girls and women who are afraid and faced with unwanted babies. May I give him your name and number, Rebecca?"

"I will need guidance, Doctor Shields, if I am pregnant." Rebecca stood up next to her mother. "I will listen to what Father Benjamin has to say." Rebecca's heart started beating with anxious fear when the nurse came in and handed the doctor the test results. She watched as Doctor Shields read the results and swallowed when she looked at her lovingly, then took her hand.

"Then I am glad you are willing to hear what Zechariah has to say, because, sweet girl, you are pregnant."

Rebecca felt numb and spoke up, mostly from nerves. "By the way, Doctor Shields, my rapist lost a silver ring with a cross lying over on its side with the letters, KOTFC engraved on it." Rebecca still did not trust Eric Shields. "Have you ever seen your husband wear a ring like that?"

"I'm sorry, Rebecca, I cannot imagine Eric wearing a ring like you described." She opened the door to see them out. "Good luck, Rebecca. If you need me, please call." After she closed the door, Janet wondered why she had just lied again for her husband. Eric did belong to an Atheist group, called the Knights of the Fallen Cross, and he wore a ring like Rebecca had described whenever he went to their annual convention in Salem, Mass. Janet had never seen Eric wear the ring any other time.

She shook her head to clear it. "Eric loves me! He would never betray our marriage! This is just a coincidence, that's all." She smiled "It could be any one of Eric's Knights of the Fallen Cross friends he goes to Salem with." She called for her next patient.

Chapter 10

"Victoria, I got your message. Please have a seat." Janet Shields had known Victoria Sinclair ever since she started her practice on Fifth and Vine. "Try to relax, we will find out the test results soon."

"I cannot believe I forgot to take my birth control pills Janet." The beautiful blonde was obviously upset. "I feel so stupid! I pride myself for knowing the facts! That is what a news anchor does! If I'm pregnant, it could ruin my career, the one thing I can count on!"

"The father of this baby, if there should be a baby, will he support you, Vicky? Perhaps, do the right thing and marry you?" this was the second unwanted pregnancy in her short day.

"Janet, he does not even want children. He has expressed that to me on several occasions." Vicky rung her hands nervously. "How can I possibly keep it! Both my career and my relationship with the man I love will be totally destroyed if I keep this baby!"

"So, we are pretty sure about being pregnant then?" Janet could feel movement from her own baby. The difference was, she was excited about having her little baby boy and she felt sure Eric was too.

"The fact points out that conclusion, Janet and between this baby and Bud, plus my career, I have no choice." Victoria and Eric had come up with nick names for each other to keep their relationship a secret. Eric had convinced her it was the right thing to do, since she had her career to think about and his teaching young adults could prove awkward if he were found having an affair. Victoria had never length Eric with Janet Shields because she knew she was happily married and most recently expecting a baby, welcome by both mother and father. Besides telling Vicky about having a good marriage and their joys of having a baby, she never heard Janet Shields speak about her personal life and she referred to her husband as Mr. Shields.

Victoria sit up when the nurse walked in with the test results, positive. Victoria broke down in tears as her friend and doctor tried to comfort her.

"Vicky, I have a good friend. His name is Father Zechariah Benjamin. He helps women through their decisions about their unwanted babies. Let me give him your name and number."

"He will probably preach to me about the wrongs of having an abortion, Janet." Vicky glanced up as she blew her nose. "I think it would be a waste of his time if I met him and my mind is already made up."

"Vicky, Zech will not tell you what to do and he does not preach to anyone. He will never judge you if you choose to have an abortion. Zech only wants to help you make sure that is the road you want to take. Vicky, perhaps you feel now that abortion is the only way out of the trap, but you need to make sure you're are making the right choice for you. Not for Bud, not for your career, but for you, Vicky Sinclair. He will not try to talk you out of your choice my friend. Zech merely wants to speak on the behalf of God."

Doctor Shields had love written on her face as she spoke to her friend. "Please Vicky, just go when he calls. Just listen to what he has to say." Janet touched Victoria's hand gently. "Do it for me, please."

"If it means that much to you, Janet, then I will go and listen to Father Zech Benjamin when he calls." Vicky got up and hugged her friend and doctor. "Pray for me Janet."

"You know I will, Vicky." Janet returned her hug and she walked with her to the door. "I think the Lord would love to hear a prayer from you as well." She winked. "And put in a good word for my baby boy, that his busy father takes time for him when arrives and loves him."

"Alright, I can do that." Victoria laughed softly. "I am sure

Mr. Shields will be crazy about his little boy, just like he is you, my dear friend." She gathered her things and left the office, passing another patient coming in the door.

Regina had been sitting quietly, waiting for her doctor to return with information on an abortion clinic, for some reason, the door that connected the two, examining room together was slightly ajar and she could hear a doctor and her pregnant patient speaking softly to one another. Not wishing to overhear a private conversation, Regina got up to close the door when the word abortion was spoken. She could hear whom she assumed was the doctor, tell her patient about a Father Benjamin, who apparently helped women who found themselves pregnant with an unwanted baby.

Looking down at the lock on her side, she tried it and found it locked. Then she tried the other side's lock and found it locked as well. So how did the door open by itself? Or did it? She thought, remembering her Sunday school teacher telling her six grade class about having their own special guardian angel, to watch over them, protect and guide them throughout out their life.

"Could my guardian angel be guiding me to something or someone for help?" Regina heard talking just outside her door and knew her doctor had returned. She turned to close the connecting door and found it shut and locked. Regina backed away and quickly found her seat just as the door opened and her doctor walked inside.

Regina promised the doctor that she would read the literature carefully before deciding to carry out the abortion, but she had another appointment and she needed to run. In truth, Regina was hoping to find the patient from the connecting room and find out how she could reach this priest. She had heard her name, and knew it was Vicky, short for Victoria. She walked outside to wait for her to come out and was surprised when she recognized the famous news anchor. Before Victoria Sinclair could walk past the woman standing

51

just outside the door, Regina spoke up.

"Miss Sinclair, my name is Regina Marshall. I never meant to overhear your conversation with your doctor, but the door between our rooms came open."

"I see." Victoria opened her purse and pulled out a pen and notepad. "How much to keep this to yourself, Miss Marshall?"

"Oh no, I'm not after your money, Miss Sinclair. Nor do I wish to harm your reputation." Regina's face flushed with embarrassment. "The fact is, I find myself in the same trouble you're in and I'm searching for answers."

"Then I sorry I jumped to the wrong conclusion, Regina, wasn't it?" Vicky put out her hand and smiled warmly.

Regina returned her smile, feeling relieved over the awkward meeting. "Yes, Regina. May I call you Victoria?"

"You may call me Vicky. That's what all my friends call me." She motioned to an outside bench, away from the sidewalk and prying eyes and ears. "Maybe we should have our conversation at a little more private spot."

Regina followed the petite blonde to a secluded bench, nestled between tall holly bushes.

"I'm not sure if I can help you Regina. I am a mess myself." Victoria smiled weakly. "A baby was just not part of my future plans, you know."

"I know very well, Vicky. I can imagine the difficult situation you're facing in the spotlight, but it is even worse in my line of work." Regina was hoping she would not have to tell this lovely well-known Television anchor what she did for a living, but being a news person, she was sure to ask questions.

"Regina, it is obvious you know my line of work, but I will not press you to tell me what you do for a living if it makes you unconvertable." It was obvious to Regina that this news anchor was compassionate and she felt this woman would not judge her choice of careers.

"I got married right out of high school to the love of my life. We had a beautiful little girl, named Joby, after her daddy.

Michael, my husband, the light of my eyes and the joy of my heart, went to live with Jesus after saving two small children from certain death." It still felt painful to talk about that sad day and Regina could not control her tears as she continued. "Michael and I were to inherit his father's hardware and sporting store, then after Michael's death, my loving in-laws willed the business to me and Joby. Three weeks later another tragedy hit our family. Old wires caused a spark and our future dreams went up in smoke."

"Regina, I'm truly sorry that happened to you, especially after losing your Michael." Victoria put her arm around Regina to console her. "Could your in-laws not replace the business?"

"The insurance company informed Mr. Marshall he had neglected to renew the business property policy, so there wasn't enough money to rebuild and replace all the merchandise. Mr. and Mrs. Marshall had to end up selling their large home and the guest house where Joby and I lived. They moved into a small house in a retirement community, but they gave the bulk of their money to us to buy us a decent home in a safe neighborhood."

"So, you had to find another job to support you and your daughter."

"At the present time, I am working to pay my bills and save enough money to take a nursing course." Regina took a big breath. Admitting her occupation to a new friend would not be easy. "I'm not proud Vicky, but I am a high price prostitute." Instead of seeing shock on Victoria's beautiful face, Regina saw real tears fill her listers eyes.

"Regina, you want Father Benjamin to call you, to help you through this overwhelming decision." Vicky looked up into the cool Autumn sky and knew winter was near and Christmas was coming soon. A time for miracles. With sincere love, Vicky took Regina's cold hand. "We will walk this path together and pray we make the right decision."

Chapter 11

Inside the chapel of Saint Mary's Catholic Church, sat three very nervous women awaiting the arrival of Father Zechariah Benjamin. A soft-spoken nun, around 40-years-old, led the small group inside the stately chapel and went to inform the priest of their arrival.

"Victoria and Regina looked over at the shy younger women, who sat with her eyes closed and obviously praying to herself as her lips moved in soft whispers. They could tell the young teen was a Christian, displaying the gold cross that hung around her neck. Regina lend over to whisper to her new-found friend.

"Poor kid. I'm sure she is regretting her actions. Probably her boyfriend. She doesn't wear a wedding ring."

"There's a lot of that going around, Regina." Victoria Sinclair was not one to gossip and unless the frightened young lady shared her story, she would never know what happen to her. "Neither of us are married either, my friend. Not that I wouldn't marry Bud if he asked me. I would jump on the wedding bliss, but he hates children." She could see Eric's bedroom eyes mocking her. "I know what Bud would insist that I do, but the decision will be mind. Once made, I will go through with my choice. It's my body."

"My sonny boy, that's his nick-name, says he loves children, especially little girls." Regina smiled as his handsome face came into view. "I suppose he told me that just to butter me up when I told him about Joby. I would marry Sonny in a heartbeat, if he asked me."

All three women looked up when the door opened and the nun walked back inside followed by a very handsome priest in his twenties. His green eyes drew their attention, along with his warm genuine smile and soothing voice.

"Welcome Victoria, Regina, and Rebecca. I am happy you came this morning to share in what I call, making the right decision for God and yourself." The priest pulled a chair up close to them and turned to the nun. She stepped forward and sit down while he brought another chair up next to her and took his seat.

"We are joined together to help lift the burden that has been placed upon you. Now, each of you must make a choice. No two cases are alike, but in the end, they are exactly alike. I asked you to send me something about your life and how you got pregnant in the first place." He laughed softly, which made him even more handsome. "Not the actual act that got you pregnant, that one is obvious. The thing we need to know is what led up to the act. I asked if each of you had informed the baby's father you were carrying his baby and other similar questions, to get acquainted with your situation. Then at the bottom of the last page, I ask if I could share anything you had written with our small group. I'd like to thank you all for saying yes." His eyes fell on Regina.

"No one in this room will judge you, Regina, for your chosen occupation. Like our Lord Jesus said, 'He who is without sin, cast the first stone. I think you would all agree, according to scripture, we have all sinned and fallen short of our own salvation." He reached over and touched her hand, as his voice came out soft and sincere. "Would you care to tell us a bit about yourself and how you ended up with this unwanted baby?"

"I have been working at Sadie's Ladies for over five years, to support me and my daughter, Joby, and to save enough money to go into nursing full time." Regina looked down, to avoid the eyes watching her as she confessed "I am a prostitute and this is the second time I have slipped up and gotten pregnant. As you can imagine, there is no room in a hooker's life for carrying a baby full term." She lifted her face slowly and noticed each person was watching her. "My first slip up

was caused by a missing pill and that led to my first abortion."
Regina noticed sadness on those around her as she continued.
"This time I got pregnant from a client I really care about and
have feelings for. It was one of my lucky weeks when Sonny
was my only customer for three days, but I forgot to take my
morning after pills those three mornings after, and I got
pregnant."

Regina could feel tears coming in her eyes as she looked
into the priest's green eyes. "Father Benjamin, I know it's not
right to have another abortion, but this baby has come at a bad
time in my life."

"Thank you, Regina, for sharing those things with us. I
know it wasn't easy." Father Benjamin patted her hand then
turned to the pretty news anchor. "Would you care to share
your story with the group, Victoria?"

"Most of you know I am the news anchor on XYII, from
6:00 to 7:00, then 11:00 till 12:00, each night, during the week.
I have been secretly seeing the most charming man who came
into my life, would you believe the food market, in the wine
section. For some unknown reason, the heavy workload,
staying constantly busy, I forgot to take my birth control pills
for the entire month of November. Bud, my boyfriend, does
not want any children and although he speaks his love for me,
he has never brought up marriage. If this pregnancy got out in
the tabloids, my reputation and career would be affected, even
ruined. People would smile to my face and whisper behind my
back." Victoria's sincere look fell on the priest. "I will listen
to what you have to say, Father Benjamin, with an open heart,
then I will make my decision."

"That is all I can ask of you, dear one." After given
Victoria a gentle pat on her arm, the priest turned his attention
on Rebecca, who had been taking in the other two women's
words, completely different from her situation. Zechariah
gathered both her hands in his and looked warmly into her
eyes. "Rebecca, I know this will be a little harder for you to

56

share with us, my child, so if you prefer, I can speak for you."

"That is very thoughtful, Father Benjamin." Rebecca spoke softly but calm as continued. "I have been in much prayer and the Lord has given me the strength I need to speak about what happen."

"God bless you, Rebecca." Zechariah reached over, patted her shoulder, then sat back in his chair and waited patiently for her to begin.

"I am pregnant because I was raped." The other two women listening, let out a gasp from her revelation. "I have no idea who raped me. It was dark and he was very cunning and knew things spoken to me from six men I am acquainted with. I have ruled out two of those men, thank God. My father and our handyman Buck."

"What kind of animal would set up innocent men?" Regina listened, eyes wide with unbelief that any human could be so cruel.

"A very smart conniving predator who knew how to stay back and learn everything he needed to know to carry out his evil plan." The priest remained calm. "This person is very intelligent who has the capability of tricking others to feed him information." The priest scooted his chair up close to Rebecca and took her hands again. "I am afraid this man is obsessed with you, Rebecca and would stop at nothing to have you. So, he waited for the perfect opportunity. It fell in his lap when your parents and the handyman were out of town and you were left alone."

"He did sound very sure of himself and extremely intelligent." Rebecca felt a chill run down her neck, just recalling the intruder. "I don't know very much about…making love, but this man knew what he was doing. He was slow in his acts, except the actual raping, he was aggressive and…I guess I should have saved some kind of evidence, like the sheets, but I did find a ring with a side way cross on top and the letters KOTFC stamped on the inside."

"A ring with a cross lying on its side?" Victoria sit up "Bud has a ring like that. There could be at least twenty men in this town that wears one. It's some kind of private club he belongs to called Circles of Faith. I'm not sure what the KOTFC stand for, but I've never seen it off his finger.

"Well, this rapist did not sound religious at all." Rebecca wanted to move on and off this evil man. "I am a freshman at Maglen University and my main major is voice and singing."

"Perhaps you will sing for us one day, my dear." The nun said softly. "I have always loved to sing myself." Rebecca smiled at the woman with the radiant smile.

"Alright ladies, we have heard from each of you and why you are struggling with this decision, whether to keep this gift or throw it away." The three women looked at one another, obviously confused by his choice of words. "I see you do not see this baby as a gift but an unwanted package you did not send for. Please hear me out before you judge the fate of this innocent baby, who is as much a victim as you are." Father Benjamin looked over at the silent nun and nodded his head and she stood up to speak.

"I speak better on my feet." Came a much stronger voice than earlier. "before I became a nun, I was a simple fifteen-year-old who enjoyed listening to my records, reading Nancy Drew Mysteries and I really had a giant crush on my next-neighbor, Jason Kertland. Jason, by the way, was nineteen and did not even know I existed." The three women listening, smiled as they tried to imagine this sweet nun doing the things she had told them. "My life changed dramatically one afternoon while walking home from school. I was grabbed into some bushes along the road, by a stranger passing through our town. He said he had been watching me and waiting for me to be alone. My best friend who lived near my house, walked home with me every evening after school, except for that day, she had soft ball practice and had to stay at school. This man raped me and slapped me around, threatened he would kill my parents if I told them. He warned me he would rape me as much as he wanted to if I ever said anything."

The group sat quietly, horrified for this sweet nun who had obviously found peace with what had happened to her.

"I found myself pregnant and did not know who to turn to. I was a good Catholic girl, so I went to my priest to confess to him in private. Father Tutland was a God sent gift who told me I must keep the baby, for its innocents was pure. I did have my little one and my parents lovingly raised him and brought him up in the faith." She looked around at the three women, love radiating from her as she said with a firm voice. "My dears, if I would have had an abortion, Father Zechariah Benjamin would not be here. He is my innocent little boy, my precious gift."

All three pregnant women sit up and looked lovingly into the green eyes of the handsome priest.

"This has come as a revelation to you ladies, that Sister Anne Marie is my mother and it is because of the choice she made twenty-five-years ago, I am alive. It is one of our sole missions on earth to help women like yourself, decide which choice is right for you." The priest bent over toward the women and held out his hands. "These babies you carry is helpless and cannot defend for themselves. They feel protected in their mother's womb, placed there by mistake, but none the less, they are living souls. The moment a baby is conceived, God gives it a living soul. It begins in heaven and by choice, could be returned.

Rebecca is a victim, the baby she carries is a victim. Victoria and Regina, you both feel trapped by your unwanted baby, but your babies are the victims, even more than yourselves" Father Benjamin reached out to all three women. "I am God's voice. When the Almighty God places a soul into a baby who has been sown, He already has plans for that child. God gives each of us gifts. Some more than others. Each one of you are carrying a child of God who even at this stage of its

59

life, has been blessed with a special gift. If you have an abortion, then you destroy the chance for that little soul to grow to be what God had planned for him or her. If you chose life, your child, son or daughter, could become that one special scientist that find curers for death causing illnesses. That minister, blessed with the gift of bringing lost souls home to our Lord or the gifted doctor who can perform surgeries never performed before." The young priest had real tears in his eyes as he said softly

"It is your decision and only you can make it ladies, but I pray you will search your heart, pray for guidance. Whatever you choose, we will not judge you. Whatever the case, we will see you through. If you choose life and wish to keep your gift, we will stand by you until the baby is delivered, if you want our help.

Remember the words of King David, Psalm 139:13: 'You created my inmost being, you knit me together in my mother's womb'." Zechariah Benjamin stood and help the three ladies stand.

"Remember God will reveal to you what to do, sometimes in ways we do not always understand at first. Listen to your heart, you then will know what He is telling you." Father Benjamin walked them to the door and gazed down into their eyes.

"Go, my sisters, and make your decisions. Sister Anne Marie and I will be praying for you until we meet again on Saturday morning for your answers. God go with you."

Chapter 12

Rebecca knew when she walked out of the chapel what her decision would be. Being a good Christian girl, she knew there was only one choice, life for the innocent baby. It did not ask to be put there any more than she ask to be raped. Rebecca would take one day at a time and except things as they fell. She knew God would be beside her all the way. Her parents would stand behind her and give her all the support they could and there was always Father Zechariah Benjamin, staying by her side until her baby was born.

Rebecca closed her eyes and smiled as the handsome face and emerald green eyes came into her vision.

Father Benjamin sat staring out his office window as his mother, sister Anne planned the next meeting with the three pregnant women they had spoken to that morning.

"Zech, I think Regina and Victoria may struggle with their decisions. I feel their careers may be their hard mountain to climb." She waited for his response, then looked up at her son. "Zech, did you hear anything I just said?"

"What?" he turned to face her. His mind had been far away on other things. She repeated her statement to him. "Mother, all these women have faith in God. They are true believers and if they pray for help, then God will reveal to them what they should do."

"Then you think God will lead them to keep these innocent ones and they will obey His will?" the nun smiled. "I pray they will listen to his call and do what is right. I believe young Rebecca is a far different case."

The young priest looked down and smiled, as his eyes lit up at the very mention of her name. Without looking at his mother, he asked "And what is your opinion about Rebecca?" Zechariah's heart felt warm just saying her name out loud and wondered to himself. "What is happening to me? Why was I lost moments ago, over that girl?"

"Are you listening to me, son?" Sister Anne reached over and touched his knee, causing him to look up at her and smile.

"Yes mother, I heard you. You think Rebecca will choose life for her baby." The young handsome priest took his mother's hands and squeezed them gently. "Mother, Rebecca has already chosen life. I could see her answer written on her beautiful face."

"Rebecca is a lovely Christian girl. She will make some man a good faithful wife one day." Anne Marie thought she noticed a slight frown fall over her son's face. "Wouldn't it be wonderful is she met a fine young Christian man, fell in love and got married so the baby could have a father to look up to."

"Mother, we cannot assume there is any such man in Rebecca's life and I won't be any part of playing match maker where Rebecca is concerned." Zechariah recreated his remarks came out so sharp. His sudden feelings for Rebecca was weighing heavy on his mind. Could he be falling in love with her or was he already there?"

A woman with an unwanted baby was one problem Father Benjamin could help solve, but a priest finding himself in love with a woman could be a big challenge and a choice he would have to make, if he was fortunate enough to have Rebecca's love in return. The young priest had two options, to pray for strength to walk away from his strong feelings or to trust those feelings that God was leading him down a different path.

For now, Father Benjamin would keep his feelings within himself until he prayed for an answer. Then wait and listen for that still small voice to guide him in the way he was to go.

Chapter 13

Regina Marshall sit at her kitchen table drinking her first cup of coffee. The house was still quiet because her little girl was still in bed asleep. Unable to get interested in the morning news, Regina switched off the television and glanced out at the sunrise, coming over the trees that rose in the distance. Her thoughts went back to the dream that woke her up at six o'clock. The dream had been so real. She could almost reach out and touch Michael. How handsome and alive he was, standing among thousands of flowers, the colors of the rainbow. In her dream she had not noticed at first that Michael wasn't alone until he said

"I brought someone to meet you, darling."

She stepped up into the light that radiated around Michael. Such a pretty little girl, around three years old. Her long blonde hair fell in waves around her cherub face and her smile was as bright as a twinkling star.

Michael placed his hand on her wavy locks and smiled at Regina. "My little friend here has been asking questions about you ever since she arrived back here some three years ago. This sweet angelic child never got to see the earth like we did, Regina. Her life was cut short before she could start growing into the beautiful child she has become."

Regina remembered feeling anxious about this little girl as she thought, this is not just some child Michael took under his wing. There was something familiar about her looks and she remembered asking Michael who this child was and why was she asking questions about her.

"This friend of yours, Michael, is she more than just a friend?" Michael's warm smile was as she always remembered whenever he tried to help or comfort her. His voice came soft as he spoke.

"This is our daughter, Regina, the one I tried to get you to keep with you. I named her Margaret."

"Oh Mike, you named her after my dear mother." Regina remembered crying in her dream and speaking. "You called her our daughter."

"She is part of you, Regina, so that makes her a part of me." He rubbed his hand over her blonde head playfully, causing her to laugh. "See darling, she has your blonde hair, while our Joby has mine, black as the ace of spades."

"Michael...Margaret, mama is so sorry baby girl." Regina remembered her tears falling in great drops down her chin and then the sweet voice of her child.

"Don't cry mama. I'm very happy in heaven, although, I miss my sister and I will miss my baby brother, Michael."

"Michael? Baby brother?" Regina repeated the words as she recalled her dream.

"He is a victim too, sweetheart. An innocent baby, whose little soul was waiting for loving parents." She remembered Michael and Margaret beginning to fade, as she heard her Michael say "Do it for Margaret, do it for me, do it for the Holy Family and most important Regina, do it for yourself and our son! Things will work out for you when you do God's will."

Absent mindedly, Regina poured herself another cup of the steaming black coffee. With those last words, Michael had vanished and she had awakened, her eyes wet with real tears. As she sat there day dreaming, Regina did not notice her six-year-old climbing up on the stool across the table. She opened the cereal box and poured some in her bowl. "Good morning mama. You want me to get the milk?" Regina got up and walked to the refrigerator for the milk and smiled back at her beautiful daughter.

"Good morning darling. Here's your milk." Regina poured the milk over the cereal, then replaced it before sitting at the counter with her daughter, coffee in hand. "You are up early, young lady. Did I forget you have to be somewhere this morning?"

"Nope! Just grandpapa's later." She took a big mouthful of her favorite cereal. "I guess my happy dream woke me up."

"A dream?" Regina knew her little girl had dreams about puppies, cute kittens and sometimes a pink horse with wings. "So, what did you dream about this time Joby? A lost puppy or a run-away kitten that was found in a tree?"

"No, I dreamed about daddy, in heaven!" she giggled. "He came right up to me and told me he loved me lots!"

"Really?" Regina felt a chill "Your daddy used to say that to me when we were dating. He would look real serious and say: 'Regina, I love you lots!"

"Cool!" Joby took another mouthful before continuing "Then I met my secret sister in my dream. She was real pretty mama, like you." She laid down her spoon, her eyes sad as she said "My sister said she was sent back to heaven and one day, we would be together."

"Joby, did…did she tell you what her name is?" Regina held her breath as her daughter looked thoughtful and smiled.

"She sure did, mama. Her name is Margaret, just like grandma's."

Regina was sitting there thinking, there was no way both her and her daughter could dream about the same thing, when Joby blurted out

"Mama, you gotta have my baby brother, Michael! Daddy ask me to be a good big sister and help him know Jesus!"

With tears flowing, Regina remembered her prayer before she climbed in bed. "Lord, help me know what I must do. Please, show me!" Then she remembered Father Benjamin's last words as they were leaving the church.

"Remember my sisters, if you pray, God will reveal to you what to do, in ways we do not always understand at first. Listen to your heart. You will know what He is telling you."

Regina knew it might not be easy. She would lose her job,

but deep down inside, she was glad of that fact. Regina knew no matter how difficult things got, her loving God would help her through. There was only one choice for Regina Marshall and her precious little girl had said it for her. "You gotta have my baby brother, Michael!"

Chapter 14

"And that is the six o'clock news. Tune in tonight for the eleven o'clock news with my co-host, Jeffery Richerson. I will see you again Monday for the six o'clock news. Have a great weekend and goodnight."

Victoria smiled her brightest smile as the camera man counted 5,4,3,2,1. Sign off.

"Have a great weekend, Randy." She patted his cheek as she walked back to her dressing room and disappeared behind the door. Beth Riggins walked from her office and looked around.

"Randy, has Vicky left already? I was going to have a word with her."

"It's not too late Beth. Victoria just went inside her dressing room." Randy picked up his gear, left a note for the night camera man filling in for him, then grabbed his overcoat and climbed inside. "She must have forgotten something, although the only nights she rushes out on is Tuesdays and Saturdays."

"Yes, I know." Said the station director. "Vicky told me she went to the gym on those nights between newscast." She looked toward the anchor's dressing room seriously. "I think there is more than she's telling us. Something is bothering Vicky and I am her friend far more than I am her boss."

"If there is something troubling Vicky, I will more than happy to pray for complete healing, weather it is body or soul." Randy's serious eyes reflected his words. "If I can help, do not hesitate to ask me Beth. Victoria is a beautiful person, and not just on the outside."

"Thank you, Randy. We all could use a word of prayer." Beth turned and went to her friend's dressing room and knocked lightly on the door. "Vicky, it's Beth. May I come in?"

Vicky had been rinsing her mouth out from her latest bout with upset stomach. She sat down at her mirror and gazed at her reflection. Her complexion was pale as she spoke softly.

"Yes, of course, come in Beth. The door is always open to you." Immediately Beth noticed her pale complexion and place her arm around Vicky's cold shoulder.

"Vicky, you're ice cold! Alright, there is something wrong with you. I am your friend, please let me help you."

"Oh Beth, it's all so complicated. I'm not sure anyone can help me." Victoria felt as though she was at the end of her rope and one wrong move, she would slip off and start falling.

"Sometimes Vicky, when you think life is too much for you to bare, help is truly only a whisper away." Beth pulled a chair up beside her and took her hand. "Sometimes, just telling a friend, talking out your problem with someone, such as myself, helps you figure out what you must do. For others, it takes a much higher person to help. Vicky, when is the last time you stepped inside that little white church you attended so faithfully before you went off to college?"

"Father Benjamin told us, me and two other women in the same situation, to pray and ask for help from God, then God would reveal to us what to do." Vicky shut her eyes, that were weary from a lack of sleep. "He said, God may reveal his answer in ways we may not understand at first, but listen with our heart and we would know what He is telling us."

"This Father Benjamin sounds like a very wise man, Vicky." Beth touched her face lightly. "You have gotten yourself in trouble, haven't you?"

"I am pregnant, Beth! It is totally my fault, forgetting to take those stupid birth control pills for a whole month." Tears began to fall.

"For starters young lady, it is not totally your fault! The father of this baby had a great deal to do about it!" Beth took Vicky's shaking hands and looked into her eyes with compassion. "Vicky, darling, this is not the end of your life, nor your career, if handled correctly."

"Beth, I truly love Bud and would marry him in a moments time should he ask me, but…" she swallowed. "He has made it plain he does not want children. If I told him, he would insist I abort the baby."

"Fortunately for the baby, it is not his call, Vicky. What does your heart tell you to do?" Beth remain calm and soft spoken.

"I think I need to say that prayer and then pay that little white church a visit as soon as I leave here." Vicky sit straight up and smiled at her dear friend. "I believe my answer lies there. I need to lay my burdens at the feet of my Lord and do His will."

"That, young lady, is a very wise decision. To choose abortion is an easy way out for you. You can do it behind closed doors, return to work and no one would ever know. Your Bud would be satisfied then. You, on the other hand, would feel the great loss for a long while or you could choose life. You may lose Bud and that could very well be a blessing in itself, but by telling your public yourself, they would admire your faith to save an innocent child and God would rain blessings upon blessings on you."

Chapter 15

Rebecca, Regina, and Victoria sat quietly waiting for Father Benjamin to finish his prayer. Each woman had reached a decision of what they would do and after concluding his prayer with a soft amen, his green eyes looked around the small group in front of him.

"Alright ladies, I trust you have come to a decision about this baby growing inside of you." The handsome young priest faced Rebecca and smiled. "Alright child, what is the fate of your child?"

"Father Benjamin, I am hardly a child. I am but six years younger than yourself." She smiled shyly. "I have come to my decision. To be honest…" she smiled at the other two women who were watching her closely. "I decided to keep this baby the last time we met here. This child may be a part of the man who raped me, but it is also a part of me and more important still, it is a living child of God, who only knows the love of God and feels safe inside it's mother's womb. I am this baby's mother."

"God bless you Rebecca." Zechariah got up and pulled her up, then gave her a hug. It was meant to be a thankful embrace, but the young priest felt so much more and unknown to him, so did Rebecca. He stepped back to look, and found her head down, as his words came out softly. "You will 'never' be alone in this, I promise." He hugged her again then pulled away as their eyes met. This time Rebecca did not look away.

"I believe you, Father Benjamin." Rebecca suddenly felt funny calling him that when she really wanted to say, "I believe you, Zech."

Afraid his true feelings might show, he turned to Regina. "What choice have you made, Regina?"

"I prayed to God, just like you ask us, then went to bed,

hoping the morning would bring some sort of answer. The answer came in my sleep, in a very real dream." Regina went on telling the group about speaking to Michael, her loving husband, and the little girl she aborted three years earlier. She told them all the words they had spoken and telling her about the baby called Michael. How Mike had excepted Margaret, whom he named after Regina's mother and the son she was to have. Regina wiped her eyes as she continued.

"I was having my morning coffee, going over my dream, when my daughter came down and told me about a dream she had. Joby said she dreamed about her daddy, Michael, whom she had never seen on the earth. He was killed before she was born. She said Michael told her he loved her lots, the same thing he use to tell me when we were dating." Regina swallowed back more tears as she continued. Then Joby told me she met her secret sister and she describe her exactly like the little girl I saw in my dream. She knew her name was Margaret and that she had been sent back to heaven but one day they would be together." Regina stood up and walked over to the big window and looked out at the snow falling outside.

"That was when I began to think how strange that my daughter and I would have the same dream when she blurted out, 'mama, you gotta have my baby brother Michael! Daddy ask me to be a good big sister and help him know Jesus!'" Regina turned to face the young priest and found tears lacing his loving green eyes. "That is when I remembered your words. God will reveal to you what to do, in ways we do not always understand at first. Listen to your heart, you will know what He is telling you." Regina looked around at the group and found them all crying. She smiled warmly, knowing she had found new friends, "I knew my choice might not be easy. I knew I would lose my job, a job I really hated, but I knew no matter how difficult things got, God would be there to help me. My answer came from two very real dreams, sent by God and through the heart of my six-year-old daughter, when she said, you gotta have my baby brother Michael!"

Father Benjamin got back up to hug Regina and this time felt only a thankful embrace. "God bless you Regina. We will be here for you as well."

"And God bless you father, for guiding me to make the right decision." She sat down and breathed, a sigh of relief, her choice had been made.

"I am next." Victoria's eyes fell on the quiet nun. "Like you, Sister Anne, I too got my answer in church. I had not been inside that little white church for years, but everything still looked the same, so it felt like coming home. I was still a member and sent my offering in the mail faithfully, once a month." Victoria got up and walked around slowly as she continued.

"Maple Grove Baptist Church had been my home church ever since I can remember and one of my favorite preachers was Reverend Joseph Taylor. I remember Reverend Taylor and his wife Doris came to Maple Grove when I was ten-years-old. I learned later from my mother, that Reverend Taylor had preached a revival at Maple Grove before I was born. The congregation loved his preaching and managed to get him when our older preacher retired." Victoria turned and smiled down at the group. "I hope I'm not going back too far in my life, but believe me, there is a reason."

"We have all day, Victoria." Sister Anne finally spoke, then smiled. "Say whatever is on your mind, my dear." Vicky looked around at the listeners.

"Thank you all for listening with such patience. Now, where was I, when I arrived at church to pray that evening after work, I found people inside having some sort of meeting with their new minister. I slipped in on the back pew, hoping no one would notice me, nor did I wish to interrupt their meeting. To my disappointment, Vera Hunter recognized me on her way out and was all hugs and kisses. Everyone at Maple Grove are loving people and Vera is one of the best at showing it. She invited me, actually, she pulled me to the front of the church to meet the new minister, after I told her I had come to pray for a friend who was in trouble. Not only is Vera loving, she has been known to gossip." Victoria had an art of telling a story, even if it was her own, that kept her audience listening.

"To be honest, I was a bit upset that Reverend Taylor wasn't still there. I could always talk to him, like another father. I was quite surprised to find Eli Spilman so handsome and young, for a minister. He kindly helped me pray for my so call friend. It was after everyone left and we were alone at the altar, that I confessed the prayer was actually for me. He just smiled warmly and we knell back down. I poured out my heart to God, telling him about Bud, about him not wanting children, about my career and my prodigal daughter act, making excuses not to attend church. Now I messed up. Forgot to take my birth control pills and got pregnant. Help me Lord, I cried. Do I abort this helpless baby or keep it?" Victoria took a deep breath and continued.

"I could feel Reverend Spilman staring at me as I prayed and when I stopped speaking, he put his arm around my shoulder and said, 'Victoria, there is someone here I think can help you.' I looked into his eyes, he was not judging me and I only saw love as he helped me up and turned me around to see my dear friend, Reverend Taylor standing behind me. He had heard my prayer and he took both my hands and led me to a seat at the front of the church.

"Vicky, I was never to tell you this child, but under the circumstances, your dear departed mother would not mind."

"Then I ask Reverend Taylor what he knew and then he told me that 'long years ago I came to Maple Grove to lead a week revival. Your mother went to the altar that night and prayed her heart out. She did realize everyone had left, so I dismissed the regular minister and went to your mother. She was only sixteen-years-old as she kneeled there and told me she had gotten pregnant by her fiancée, Victor McBride. She

73

had made love to Victor the night he left to fight in the Vietnam War. The day she received word that Victor had been killed was the same day she found out she was pregnant. I told your mother that I knew she was scared, needed to finish school, but I also told your mother that this baby was all that was left of her Victor, for her and his parents. I also remember telling Ruth, that this child she carried was a child of God, whose life was already laid out for it, from God himself.'"

Vicky swallowed. "I remember Reverend Taylor had tears to match mine as he continued. 'Your mother had that baby Victoria. It was a little girl, you.' I grabbed my chest and let out the words: my mother was in the same situation as I was and I could have been aborted. As I wept, Reverend Taylor said 'Yes Vicky, she was thinking about having an abortion but she didn't. Do you remember how you mama always called you Vic? That was short for Victor and it was what she always called him. She named you Victoria, after your father, so she could call you Vic. A part of him, the man she loved. Now you are facing the same decision Vicky. This child you are carrying could be as special as you are.' I was crying so hard I could hardly see, but I knew Reverend Spilman was standing there and I could see tears in his eyes as well." Victoria took a deep breath.

"Of course, I chose life for this baby. And like they say, when God closes one door, he opens a window. Reverend Taylor saw me out last night and I told him how sad I was that he was leaving Maple Grove. He assured me he would not be going anywhere. Maglen was his home and Maple Grove was his church. He had retired but agreed to fill in for brother Spilman whenever he needed him." She laughed softly to herself. "My old friend told me if my future did not work out with Bud, he could set me up with a great guy. I ask him if he were in the match making business and he remarked, only for a few friends who were special to him. Then I ask him who he had in mind and he simply said, why our new minister. He said he thought he was waiting for the right girl and he thought that could easily be me."

"And what did you say to that, Vicky?" Regina could not hold back another second.

"I informed Reverend Taylor, that if things did not work out for me and Bud, I would be calling." Victoria felt better after telling her story. "There was something about Eli that caught my eye, I must admit."

"Ladies, you have made a wise choice and I'm proud of all of you." Father Benjamin got up to hug Vicky. "These doors are always opened to you."

"Thank you, father, Sister Anne. It really was you who started my heart to think." Vicky patted Regina's hand "Want to have some lunch with me?" she turned to Rebecca. "You too dear. I would love to treat you both."

"Thank you kindly, Vicky, but mother is expecting me home for lunch. Maybe another time." Rebecca stood up and hugged her and Regina then turned to leave when Father Benjamin stopped her.

"Rebecca, I hear you are singing Sunday at your church. I hope you don't mind if I attend to listen."

"That is very sweet of you father. You are always welcome at Sunny Side Methodist Church." Rebecca smiled brightly. "If you can, we would love for you to come to our home for lunch after church. Mama and daddy have heard me speak about you so much, they would love to meet you."

"If it would be no trouble." His smile matched hers.

"No trouble at all, father." Rebecca felt like laughing with joy.

"Then, I will be there Rebecca." He took her hand. "I look forward to spending my Sabbath with you."

Rebecca smiled with complete happiness as she walked to the door, then turn back to say

"I look forward to it as well, Zech." She turned and raced out the door, feeling like singing with total joy.

Chapter 16

Victoria had planned for the worst with Eric after she told him about the baby. As always, Eric stood smiling as he lifted up the bottle of expensive wine.

"My dearest Victoria, I have brought an extra special bottle of wine tonight, so we can celebrate my good news!"

"Good news?" Victoria took the bottle and walked over to open it.

"Yes darling. I will be able to come over more often now! Doesn't that sound wonderful?" he walked over to the cabinet and took out two wine glasses.

"Just set them down Bud and if you will, pull the lasagna out of the oven while I pour the drinks." Vicky filled his glass with the wine then poured herself a glass of grape juice and set them on the table as she got the salads.

"Vicky, you have not commented about my good news, darling." Eric set the hot dish on the table then sampled the wine and smiled as he watched Victoria take her seat. "Have you had a chance to sample the wine yet? I'm sure you will like it."

"I am sure it is very good wine Bud. You really know your wine." She waited for him to sit, then she lifted her glass and took a sip of the juice.

"Well, what is the verdict, my dear?" Eric smiled as he took another sip. "Was I right?"

"For grape juice, it is very delicious, darling." Victoria returned his smile as he stared over at her perplexed.

"Grape juice? Boy, that's an insult on fine Italian wine!" he frowned.

"Bud, I too have good news to share with you." Victoria noticed Eric turning pale as he wondered, surely it could not have happened to both my women.

"By all means Vicky, tell me your good news."

"Bud, we are going to have a baby." She waited for a moment for his response but there was only silence. "I know you said you wanted our relationship to be just the two of us and children was something you did not want."

"You knew this Vicky, then why in God's name, did you get pregnant? I thought you were taking birth control pills!" Eric eyes shot fire as he lifted his wine and drank it down.

"I was on birth control pills Bud, but for some reason, I simply forgot to take them for solid month." Vicky remained calm because she had braced herself for any reaction from Eric.

"Alright Victoria, so you made a stupid mistake, but we can easily take care of it!" Eric walked over to her desk drawer and pulled out the phone book. "Look Vicky, I will pay whatever it cost to have an abortion, but that baby has got to go or…"

"Or what Bud?" Victoria pushed her chair back and grabbed the phone book from Eric. "Are you threating to leave me if I chose to have this baby?"

"Look Vicky, this fetus is little more than an egg, its not a baby yet!" he almost shouted, as he felt his safe sex world was cashing in around him. "Vicky, if you care anything for me, get rid of this damn baby!"

"For starters Bud, this baby that is growing inside of me is not just a fertilize egg. The night I conceived this baby, he or she received a soul from God in heaven!" Victoria had often wondered about Eric's faith. Now she felt sure she would soon discover just what he believed in or did not believe in.

"A soul? Heaven?" Eric laughed out mockingly. "Come down to earth Victoria! Aren't you a little old to believe in fairy tales? You report facts Vicky and the clear fact that you are lacking is believing in a myth that does not exist!"

"Bud, you ask me if I cared for you." Victoria walked over to the door. "I suppose I did care for you Eric before I found out how heartless and cruel you can really be!" She grabbed the bottle of Italian wine and thrust it into his hand. "Take your wine with you! I will take care of my baby, a special gift from God! You are the one with the blinders on, Eric!"

"Victoria, you are a smart, educated journalist, how can you believe in something you cannot see, touch or feel?" Eric stared down at the beautiful blonde.

"That is where faith, real faith comes in, Eric. Where seeing is believing and believing is seeing!" Victoria gave him a slight push into the hall. "Goodbye Bud. I will never stop praying for you!"

Before he could say another word, Victoria shut the door in Eric's face. Suddenly, she felt better, relieved and smiled down at the telephone, picked it up and dialed Reverend Taylor.

"Reverend Taylor, this is Vicky, are you still playing match maker?"

Chapter 17

Regina checked her reflection in the mirror one last time. Eric would be arriving any minute, ready for their usual fun night. Only this time, Regina had some news to share with the man she loved and hoped to marry as soon as she left this job for good. Now would be the perfect time to quit, she thought, and marry Eric, have their baby then start nursing school.

Eric had told her more than once, he loved kids, so she felt good about what she was about to spring on him. The soft knock came on the door. She quickly brushed down her nervous feeling and opened the door and saw his handsome smile and his hand holding up a bottle of French wine.

"Sonny! Just on time, as usual." She joined him in a kiss as he shut the door and laid the bottle of wine in his palm for her to examine.

"I think you will enjoy this selection my beautiful Regina." He walked over to the table set ready for dinner except for the fact that there was just one wine glass sitting out, at his seat. "Darling, did you forget your wine glass?"

"I'm having water tonight, sweetheart." She let him pull the chair out for her as he always did. "You enjoy the wine, I'm sure it is perfect."

"Why aren't you drinking tonight, dearest? Do you have an interview bright and early for nursing school?" he easily pulled out the cork and poured himself a generous glass.

"No Eric, but I do have some wonderful news. You might need to take a deep breath and a big sip." She teased.

"You have my attention Regina. What has got you so excited?" Eric took a small sip, then a little more, before saying "Mumm, this wine is excellent Regina. Are you sure you won't have just a small glass?"

"After I tell you the joyful news, I know you will understand why I choose to have water instead of wine."

Regina was beaming with total happiness as she waited for Eric to respond. Eric swallowed, as the reality of what she was trying to say to him hit. In the heated moment, Eric turned up his glass and emptied the contents into his mouth before pouring his glass full. He looked at Regina and faked a smile.

"Do continue Regina. Don't keep me in suspense if the news is that wonderful."

"Sonny, we are going to have a baby!" Regina almost sang it out. "Isn't that beautiful darling?" Instead of seeming happy, she noticed his frown and the redness on his face.

"Regina, how the hell did that happen? I thought you were taking morning after pills! Did you deliberately miss those pills?"

"No, I just forgot to take them, darling. I guess it was all the excitement of being with only you last week." Regina couldn't understand Eric's outburst when she told him. Sure, the facts could have brought on shock but not anger, if he really loved her as he claimed. He looked at her with discuss and coldness as his words came out harsh.

"How can you be sure this baby is even mine? After all, you have sex with many men, being a paid prostitute!" he almost shouted.

"I am sure, Eric, this baby is yours! Up until last week, I was taking those darn pills! The only time I did not take them was after my nights with you!" Regina felt hurt that he would think of her as only a prostitute. "I thought you really cared for me! Led me to believe we had a future together! How could I be so stupid!"

Eric got up and pulled her up into his arms as his lips brushed across her ear "Regina darling, I do care about you. I'm sorry I sounded so harsh. It all came as a shock to me, so sudden." He buried his face in her good smelling hair. "I just need time to adjust to becoming a parent. Will you forgive me my dearest?"

"Oh, Sonny, of course I forgive you. I knew it would be a

shock. Believe me, it was a shock I wasn't expecting either. But then, I remembered you saying how much you love children so I thought you wouldn't mind becoming a father."

"And you're right, I do love children, Regina, but can I love you a little more?" Eric's lips melted over hers in a fiery kiss as he picked her up and carried her to bed where they made passionate love.

Eric kissed Regina goodnight and told her he would see her on their night unless he had exam papers to finish grading. Regina fell asleep, happy that everything was going to work out.

Regina had canceled all the other customers to devote her time to the father of her baby. So, the evening finally rolled around for them to be together. She could not wait to see him and was certain from his reaction at their last meeting, the baby would be excepted with joy. The knock came on her door, a few minutes earlier than usual and she thought Eric was to happy to wait. Regina opened the door smiling, expecting to see her 'sonny' holding his bottle of wine. Instead, she saw her employer, Sadie.

"Regina dear, may I come in? I need to talk with you."

"Of course, Sadie." Regina stepped back so she could enter and looked up the empty hall before shutting her door. "Sadie, Eric will be here soon. What is this about?" Regina felt butterflies creeping in her stomach, knowing her boss had never disturbed her this close to a client's coming.

"My dear, it is about Mr. Wexford that I am here. He won't be coming tonight." Sadie's eyes held sadness as she watched Regina's face fall. "He called just minutes ago."

"He did say he might have exam papers to grade." Regina had one small hope. "I guess he didn't know until the last minute that he could never finish on time."

"Regina" Sadie took her hand. "Mr. Wexford ask to be dropped from your list. He won't be coming back to you, my dear."

81

"Dropped?" Regina felt her heart racing. "He...won't be coming back?"

"No child. He said he had moved in with his mother to take care of her and he wouldn't have any free time for himself." Sadie shook her head in discuss. "Forgive me Regina, but I believe the bastard is lying. He checked out Tracy and Monica before leaving last time he was here. I am pretty sure he will be calling for one of them soon."

"Then, you are saying, Eric was just using me, for sex?" Regina felt sick.

"Regina, like most of these men, they use undercover names, as not to be traced. Most of them are married, therefore, they are incapable of becoming attached to you. When things run smooth for them, they act as though they are in love with you and in some cases, even pretend to like your children." Sadie took a big breath, knowing Regina had fallen in love with this Eric. "Regina, I really think Mr. Wexford did have a thing for you, darling and it was mostly the sex you shared. When you told him you were pregnant, he saw his perfect life with you torn apart, so he ran. It's my guess that he is married and could have never married you anyway, Regina."

"Life has its lessons, Sadie." Regina wiped her tears away and looked down at the dinner he had ordered going cold. "I can live without Sonny, but I cannot live without my children, Joby, Margaret, and Michael Jr. Its them I'll be living for now."

Sadie did not know how this beautiful girl was going to pay for her dream of becoming a nurse if she had bills to pay and no income coming in. She said sadly

"All the clients are with the other girls tonight, darling. If you wish to wait around, we might have a drop in."

"That won't be necessary Sadie." Regina stood tall, picked up her glass of water and took a big sip. "I am turning in my resignation. This is my last night playing the harlot."

"Regina, what will you do, child? You have bills to pay and I know you haven't saved enough money yet for nursing school." Sadie was genially concerned for her.

"I will look for work to do, first thing in the morning, dear friend and I have all that money I've put back for nursing school. I can use it if I need to. I will not let my child go hungry."

"Then come by my office in the morning Regina. You can pick up your final check and there will be some extra in there for you." Her boss and friend gave her a big hug. "If you need a friend or a shoulder, I will always be here for you. Regina."

"Thank you, dear friend. I will always love you." Regina returned her hug, then pulled out her large luggage to pack. She smiled at Sadie as she walked to the door. "Sadie, you are the best!"

Chapter 18

Rebecca waited nervously with the choir before entering the sanctuary. It was not just her solo that had her apprehensive, it was the fact that Father Benjamin was sitting out in the congregation. She had a chance to peek out earlier to look for him and spotted him on the third row facing the choir loft, chatting with Olive Porter, one of the widows who sit alone every Sunday.

Mr. Spangler gave the nod to precede into the choir loft where Rebecca always stood on the end of the front row, where she could easily slip out for her solo's. Her eyes locked with the handsome priest and a smile fell on both their lips. During the service, their glances came frequent and Rebecca realized her true feelings for this man. She had fallen in love with him.

When the minister began reading the scripture, Rebecca slipped to the back to prepare for her solo. She closed her eyes and whispered a soft prayer before going out.

"Lord, take away any fear I have and give me a strong, clear voice, to sing for your glory." Rebecca walked to the door that would take her back out into the sanctuary and the waiting silent congregation. She picked up her microphone as the piano player started the introduction. As expected, Rebecca sang from her heart, to the Lord she loved and served. Her angelic voice rang out "Breath of Heaven" as her eyes were fixed on the screen in front of her, revealing the Virgin Mary and her son, Jesus, the Christ child. When she finished singing, she heard the strong, yet familiar, amen. Rebecca gazed into his beautiful emerald green eyes and smiled beautifully as joy filled her heart. She looked out at all the teary faces and knew her church family had felt the presence of God.

Father Benjamin found the choir room after church and was waiting outside the door for Rebecca when Nancy rushed past him, still dressed in her choir robe.

"Wow! Did you guys get a good look at that handsome priest standing outside the choir room?

"I noticed him sitting out front in the congregation during the service!" Martha Fuller blushed. "He could sing real pretty. It's too bad he has to be a priest! He is one doll of a man!"

Rebecca smiled as she slipped on her coat. "I got to run girls. My guest is waiting for me." Nancy grabbed her arm and pulled her around.

"Bec, are you telling us, that handsome priest is out there waiting for you?"

"Exactly Nancy, and it is not polite to keep him waiting." Rebecca hugged her shocked friends "See you Friday evening at choir practice. I'm off!"

"But...Bec? Where...?" Nancy and Martha watched Rebecca dash out the door and took Father Benjamin by the hand, then walked quickly out the side entrance where her parents were waiting.

"Mama, Daddy, this is my dear friend, Father Zechariah Benjamin."

"It is so good to finally meet you, Father Benjamin?" Mary Bradford shook his strong hand "Our daughter has told us many wonderful things about you, father."

"You are quite young son, not anything like I pictured." John Bradford smiled as he shook his hand as well, then smiled over at his daughter. "Rebecca, sweetheart, you can ride with this fine young priest while I lead the way."

"Would you care for another piece of fried chicken, Father Benjamin?" Mary held out the large platter of fried chicken toward the young man as he waved it away, smiling.

"Everything was extremely delicious, Mrs. Bradford, but I could not possibly eat another bite right now." Picking up his glass, Zechariah drank down his iced tea, then sit back.

"Son, Rebecca made a lovely chocolate layer cake." John Bradford winked at his blushing daughter as he remembered how happy she was putting on the creamy icing, then layering each layer with walnuts. She had learned from Sister Anne, chocolate-black walnut cake was his very favorite, topped with vanilla ice cream. "Perhaps we can have cake and coffee later, after our lunch settles a bit."

Zech smiled over at Rebecca and said softly "That sounds perfect, Mr. Bradford." He touched Rebecca's hand under the table. "I look forward to this special cake."

"In the mean-time, Rebecca, why don't you take your friend to the winter porch to talk." Rebecca's mother got up and started clearing the table. "John and I will be out later with the cake and coffee."

"Thank you, mama, that sounds wonderful." Rebecca led the way out to the long warm porch, lined with large picture windows, to give the appearance that you were outside. "Here we are, father. What do you think?"

Rebecca's visitor stepped over to the windows and looked out at all the tall willow oaks surrounding a large lawn, freshly covered in white snow. The steeple of the Methodist Church rose up in the distance and a large barn sit just down a quant country road lined with large pine trees.

"Rebecca, this is as warm as a Christmas card. What a beautiful, peaceful place to come and meditate." Looking around the long porch, Zechariah spotted a swing on the far in, facing the beautiful view outside. His eyes caught Rebecca's. "Join me on the swing?"

"I'd love too." She made her way over to the large swing and sat down as the priest joined her and started swinging slowly as Rebecca touched his hand. "I'm glad you came today."

The young priest smiled brightly and took her hand. "I have been wanting to tell you, your solo this morning was beautiful, Rebecca. I've heard Amy Grant sing it, and as always, she does a wonderful job, but hearing you sing it, you sounded like a voice of an angel." Rebecca blushed from the heart felt compliment.

"God is good Father Benjamin. His blessing and gifts given are bountiful and always beautiful."

"You are a beautiful person, Rebecca Bradford. Filled with the incredible love of Christ." Father Benjamin looked deeply into her alluring blue eyes. "You will make some man a very lucky person."

"Would I?" she glanced up, her eyes filled with love.

"Is there a special person in your life, Rebecca?" his eyes held hers, as Rebecca fixed her attention directly at him.

"Yes, there is. I must confess, I have not known him very long, but I knew I had deep feelings for him the moment I saw him."

"And does he have the same feelings for you?" the young priest's heart was troubled that it might be himself she spoke about.

"I cannot be sure of his feelings for me, but I feel nothing could surely come from this love even if he felt something for me." She glanced down, unsure if she should confess her love to the man sitting next to her.

"And why is that, Rebecca? Is the man you speak of already married?" Zechariah knew he was pushing his way into her private life, but his feeling for her was obvious to him. He was in love with her.

"In a way, he is married, Father Benjamin. Just not to a woman." Rebecca looked up and found him watching her closely. "He is married to his beliefs, his church, his God."

Zechariah closed his eyes knowing the truth was spoken and his words came out just above a whisper "Rebecca, this man you love, is it…?

"Yes, Zech, it is you." Their eyes met again. "I loved you from the very moment I saw you. I have to be honest with you for I have never told a lie in my life."

"Nor I Rebecca." Father Benjamin took both her hands, "For you see, I too have feelings for you. I cannot stop thinking about you. I love you, Rebecca."

"What can we do, my darling? You are a priest and have taken vows, just like your mother, a nun."

"Rebecca, my heart is to serve God always." He watched her eyes mist up and drop to her lap. He lovingly lifted her face and looked with love into her eyes. "Rebecca, my life must serve God, but I want you in that life with me, my darling, beside me, always. If that means changing my faith, then I will become a Methodist preacher."

Rebecca looped her arms around his neck. "Oh Zechariah, do you love me that much?"

"I love you more, much more!" his eyes fell on her lips. "Never in my life have I wanted to kiss a girl like I do you, my dearest Rebecca."

"There is no one stopping you, Zechariah Benjamin. My lips are yours and yours alone, my love. Kiss me!"

The young priest was new at kissing, but it came, natural as he parted his lips over the girl he loved in a passionate kiss, overflowing with new love.

"Now I know we must become one, for I have tasted your sweet lips and know this is what God has intended for us. To be united forever, my darling Rebecca."

"Zechariah, are you asking me to marry you?" Rebecca had never been happier than she was at this very moment.

"Yes, I am! Rebecca Bradford, will you marry me and permit me to be the father of this innocent baby that grows inside you?" he smiled, happy the truth was out and she felt the same incredible love for him.

Rebecca laughed with joy and threw herself into his arms. "Yes! Yes, I will marry you my dearest Zechariah!" Happy tears filled her blue eyes as she laughed happily. "This little one I carry is indeed lucky to have found such a wonderful loving daddy!"

"It is I that's lucky, Rebecca. To have found a woman with such loving faith in the Holy Family, to be at my side and sing their praises wherever our faith journey leads us." Zech pulled her into his loving arms and held her close. "Rebecca, because our engagement happened so fast and the fact that I am a priest, I just hope and pray your parents understand and except me."

"You are more than excepted, my son." John Bradford and his wife Mary, had been listening in the door way, to the last part of the young couple's conversation. "To be honest young man, you are an answer to our prayers "

"Forgive us for apparently ease dropping, but we thought cake and coffee would be pleasant out here on the winter porch's table." Mary blushed, but like her husband, she was over joyed for her daughter. "John and I have been praying that God would send a good Christian man in our daughter's life, not just for the baby but for our Rebecca as well." Rebecca's mother had twinkles in her eyes as she added "We are overjoyed that you are engaged."

"There is one small hiccup." John Bradford wrinkled his brow and Rebecca got up to hug her father.

"Daddy, I don't need a big fancy wedding. You needn't worry. All I need is Zech."

"Silly girl, your daddy is referring to college, you finishing your music degree." Mary set down the tray laden with cake, ice cream and coffee on the big long wooden harvest table, flanked by two long wooden benches.

"Mama, Zech and I will discuss what I need to do about college." Rebecca lovingly helped her mother by cutting big slices of the four-layer chocolate walnut cake and scooping vanilla ice cream over them while her mother poured fresh brewed coffee from a large silver pot into fancy cups.

"Mr. and Mrs. Bradford, I will never stand in Rebecca's way to have a singing career." The young priest had got up to place his arm lovingly around Rebecca. "Her beautiful angelic voice will be a big part of our ministry and I think religious concerts are a must for our singing angel, not to mention recordings."

"That sounds perfect for our little girl." John Bradford patted his future son-in-law's back as he ushered him over to the big long table. "Now, young man, you can sample your girls' gift for baking while we discuss our little girl's 'big' elaborate wedding!"

Chapter 19

The knock came softly on Brook Falls apartment door. She opened it smiling, knowing it would be her cousin Rebecca, who had called her earlier to inform her she had some wonderful news to share and wanted it told in person. Brook took her cousin by the hand and pulled her into the well-furnished room.

"Do come in Rebecca and tell me your news! I cannot wait a minute longer." Still clutching her hand, Brook pulled her over to a plush red sofa, made in rich soft velvet. "So, out with it, my dearest friend!"

"My dear cousin, I am engaged to be married!" Rebecca held up her left hand revealing a beautiful engagement ring adorned with a big sparkling diamond.

"Engaged? Wow, take a look at that rock!' Brook's eyes flew wide open in total shock. "You're getting married? I didn't even know you were dating! When did this all happen and who is the lucky fellow? Someone from school, perhaps."

"My future husband is no one you know, Brook. He is the most wonderful, most handsome loving man I've ever had the privilege in knowing! And to make him even more suitable for me, he is a man of faith and commitment to doing the will of our God."

"So, he is a man of God. A preacher?" Brook sat up and smiled.

"Yes, he is something like a preacher." Rebecca finally noticed her surrounding and how the large apartment was completely furnished with expensive furniture and fine pieces and paintings hanging gracefully on the rich wallpaper. She started to wonder how her cousin could afford a place like this. Rebecca also knew her first cousin personal status and couldn't see her renting or owning anything as plush as this wealthy-looking apartment. Knowing Brook was from a poor family and her only job was waiting tables a few hours a week after school hours. Brook smiled over at her friend as she watched her checking out the originals by some of the old master painters.

"Rebecca, I see you are enjoying the oil paintings and fine furnishings in my apartment. I know what you must be thinking. It looks too expensive for my pitiful income, am I correct?"

"Well, things do look like they cost far too much money for what you make unless you won a lottery dear cousin and fail to mention it to your friend and favorite cousin." Rebecca teased as Brook broke out in laughter.

"A lottery? Hardly, sweet Rebecca. It is easily explained cousin. When I rented this apartment, it came fully furnished, just as you see it. The couple I rent from are very wealthy and decided to move into a large home, so this place came up for rent. Needless to say, I feel like a queen living here."

Rebecca smiled, never doubting her cousin's honesty. They had always been close, the best of friends and went through school together every since the first grade.

"I am happy for you Brook, if you don't mine living alone."

"I have only been living here for two weeks, but I find the single life suits me. I feel free to be myself." Brook quickly changed the subject back to Rebecca's engagement. "Enough about me, tell me more about this wedding. When is the big day? After you graduate college?"

"Much sooner than graduation, Brook." Rebecca's eyes danced with joy as she sat up excited and said, "Zech and I are having a Christmas wedding!"

"Christmas? That soon? Wow! This happened real fast! Will you have a big wedding?"

"Mama has started the invitations to everyone we know, along with the entire church family. Zech offered the big

Catholic Church in the center of town if we needed someplace bigger than my church. He was as happy as I when I told him I wanted to be married in my church. Reverend Anderson is happy to perform the ceremony and the church is already adorned with Christmas!" Rebecca took both of Brook's hands in hers. I want you to be one of my bridesmaids. I will be wearing white, of course, but you along with Nancy, Martha Fuller and Jane Cook, will be wearing red and green."

"May I have red" I think I look great in red. Er...Erin told me last Christmas at church that red was my color." Brook laughed as she blushed. "I would love to be one of your bridesmaids, Rebecca. Thank you for asking me."

"Thank you for saying yes. You and Martha can wear red and Nancy and Jane can wear green, my four Christmas angels!" Rebecca stood up and slipped into her coat and scarf. "I will call you soon for the fitting." She walked to the door then hugged her cousin. "Your apartment suits you, Brook. It is beautiful, just like you! Gotta run! Love you!"

"Drive careful cousin, it's starting to snow again. I love you too!" Brook shut the door, smiling to herself, knowing he had been standing just inside their bedroom waiting for her visitor to leave.

"You may come out darling, Rebecca is gone."

"So, our little songbird is getting married." Eric Shields took around Brook's tiny waist. "I never knew our Rebecca was seeing anyone."

"To be honest Eric, I knew nothing about a boyfriend with the name of Zech and My dear cousin and I discuss everything personal in our lives. Well, not everything." She touched his handsome face and smiled, then ran her fingers through his thick dark hair. "How did you like my clever response explaining why 'my' apartment was furnished so lavishly?"

"Your quick thinking is one of the things I love about you Brook." His hand ran over her blonde hair. "Although, my cute sexy lover almost let my name slip out."

"True, my darling, but again I covered my mistake brilliantly, would you not agree, handsome?" Brook kissed his bare chest, causing Eric to take a big breath.

"Clever and seductive. I think it's time we made love."

"I am yours Eric. The bed waits." Brook moved her eyes slowly up his manly body until they landed on his bedroom eyes.

"Do you think Rebecca will continue in college or just become this wonderful man's wife?" Eric patted Brook on her rear and walked over behind the hidden bar. "She never really told you her planes for continuing her courses."

"Knowing Rebecca, she will be devoted first to her man, then her career." Brook tried never to show her jealousy over Eric obsession over her beautiful cousin. In the past, she had told him many things about Rebecca, because he had asked. Pacific things people had said to her whenever she was with her cousin, either at church, when they went shopping at the local drug store or staying over at her house, around her parents and their handy man, Buck. Eric especially wanted to know things men would say to her. Men like her daddy, Buck, Mr. Shoemaker, the pharmacist and even the preacher and choir director from their church. She never questioned him about why he wanted to know these things, even though it seemed a bit odd to her.

Brook told herself that Eric really loved her and that Rebecca was nothing more than someone he fantasized and knew he could never have. Maybe it was because Eric was not a religious man, in fact, he was an atheist. Maybe Rebecca's strong Christian beliefs sparked his interest in her and why he had gotten so mad at Brook that day in class when she spoke up for God and against him and his argument with her cousin.

She remembered Eric being cold to her that afternoon in his apartment until she swore she was only saying those things to throw her cousin off their trail, even though she knew Rebecca had no idea she was having sex with their professor.

He had remained cold to her until she denounced her faith in God and told him she would do anything for him. Then, they had had the hottest sex she could remember.

"Brook, are you listening to me darling? I ask you if you would like a glass of wine." Eric smiled and held up a bottle of French wine and two glasses. "Your mind seems to be a thousand miles away."

"You are right as usual Eric." She smiled and took the offered wine. "I was day dreaming, nothing you need to worry about. I am very much on the pill and I do not plan to get pregnant."

"If everyone was as smart and loyal as you, my Brook, my life would be easier." He bent down and kissed her. "Janet is still living in her fantasy world, believing in something and someone who has never assisted! Now she has gone and gotten herself pregnant and wants me to be happy about the brat."

"It would appear, your wife is everything you despise in a person, darling." Brook patted the sofa and moved over for him to sit down. "She believes in God and is going to have a baby, deliberately, against your wishes."

"It's true we are opposites and Janet, does things her way. She is her own person and a very successful surgeon." Eric looked thoughtful. "I don't think Janet does things to hurt me. Her love for me is strong and she loves being married to me. Janet is very happy with her life, her choices and together we bring in a handsome income I've grown accustomed to."

"I know you enjoy the finer things in life Eric, but does Janet make you happy?" Brook always knew about Janet. Even Regina Marshall and Victoria Sinclair. Eric was devoted to her and their relationship. He knew he could confide in her about anything, except, she thought, his obsession over her cousin Rebecca. So, Brook was inwardly happy Rebecca would be getting married at Christmas.

"Yes Brook, having Janet as a wife is pretty wonderful." Eric drank down his wine and checked his watch. "Speaking of my devoted wife, she will be getting home in about two hours." Eric pulled Brook up from the sofa, took her almost empty glass, finished it, then walked her to the bedroom.

"Eric, do you love Janet?" Brook pulled off her clothes and Eric pulled her close against his naked chest.

"She is beautiful, intelligent, a heart surgeon, blonde and a good lover."

"Yes, she is all those things Eric, but do you love her?" she glanced up and he noticed how serious she become and the sudden need to know. "Do you love me?"

"Brook, Brook, my beautiful sexy woman." His hand ran down her bare back causing her to breathe in. "You must know I love Janet. She is my wife." He felt her body grow stiff. "But, my darling, she is but a good lover. You are a terrific lover." Eric lifted her face, and his fingers traced her young lips. "Do I love you? Oh, my Brook, that day in the class room when you wore no panties just to turn your old man on, I wanted to walk back to your desk and lift you up, sling you on the floor, climb on top of you, then screw you! I was in torture looking at you. Seeing what I wanted but could not get it."

"Eric, I know you have got the hots for me. We are great in bed." Brook remained serious as his smile filled her with uneasiness, "Please, just answer my question. Do you love me Eric?"

"Brook, can't you tell, can't you feel?" his lips parted over hers, then brushed down her neck. "Yes, my dearest darling. I love you. I could only tell the women I love most everything about myself. No one knows the real me like you do Brook. I chose to tell you because you mean more to me than anyone else."

"Oh, Eric." Brook returned his kisses with passion. "I love you my darling. Just know you can tell me anything. I will never judge the man I love most." She whispered, as she thought about his obsession over Rebecca. "Maybe it is wondering what she might be like in bed and knowing he will never find out."

Chapter 20

Regina sat nervously outside Doctor Todd Williams' office. She had sent in a contest entry titled: "Why I would be the perfect nurse" Regina had read about the contest in the local newspaper. It appeared this doctor was reaching out to those wanting to become a nurse but did not have the means to afford the course. With the urging from her father and little girl, Joby, Regina had written her reasons for wanting to go into nursing. She had boldly confessed about her past job and the fact that she had gotten pregnant left her without an income. Through dreams and her strong faith in a forgiving Lord, she had decided to keep her baby and that would give her two children to take care of.

To Regina's surprise, she had been called in for an interview with a staff member. So here she was wondering how many other contestants had been called in for the same reason.

"Ms. Marshall, please follow me." A very kind middle age receptionist opened one of the office doors and called out softly. "Doctor Williams, this is Regina Marshall, sir."

"Regina, yes of course." The handsome doctor around fifty-years-old, arose from his leather chair and walked around his oak desk smiling, hand extending for a handshake, "Ms. Marshall, welcome to Mercy Health."

"Doctor Williams, I feel honored that you would have me come in for this interview." She shook his hand. "I felt somewhat surprised to get the call."

"Your letter was very moving and your honesty was truly refreshing." The doctor pulled out a chair for her in front of the large desk, then walked back to his seat. "I must admit it was the second letter that led me to choose you. May I call you Regina?"

"Yes, please." She looked over at him perplexed. "Forgive me Doctor Williams, but did you say the second letter convinced you? I can assure you sir I only wrote the one letter."

"I know Regina, but a very wise and caring friend who reached out to us on your behalf, wrote us a compelling letter." Todd Williams pulled out the white stationary with the cymbal of a gold cross at the top. "Father Zechariah Benjamin has written a very convincing letter stating the reason why you should receive this nursing degree." The doctor handed Regina the letter for her to read.

Regina tried to hold back her tears as she read the loving words and saw the signatures of support at the bottom. After the young priest's name came Sister Anne, then Rebecca, Victoria, her ex-boss Sadie, Mr. and Mrs. Marshall, Michael's parents, Doctor Janet Shields from Maglen Hospital, her loving father and her little daughter, Joby. Next to her daughter's name was printed, 'please let my mama win. She will make you the best nurse ever! I know, 'cause she has nurse me through the mumps and the measles! Thank you!' Regina forced a smile up at the doctor, who sat quietly, waiting for her to finish reading.

"Thank you for sharing that with me Doctor Williams." Suddenly it dawned on Regina the good doctor, had said earlier, the second letter had led him to 'choose' her. "Did…did you say, you chose me?"

"Regina, you are exactly what we have been looking for." He reached across the table and retrieved the letter. "We need someone who is dedicated to the job. Someone who will be compassionate to our patients, and who works well with other staff members. Someone who has a strong faith, a belief in God and who lives out her faith. You are that someone, Regina Marshall." His hand pressed for his secretary. "Miss Swanson, could you bring us some coffee."

"Yes, coming sir," came the respectful response.

"Doctor Williams, how can I ever thank you?" Regina looked up when the office door opened and the aroma of fresh brewed coffee filled the air. "Miss Swanson, that coffee smells heavenly."

"Thank you my dear, I do make a great brew." Smiling, the secretary placed the tray on top of the desk then poured two cups of steamy hot coffee. "Would you care for cream or sugar, Ms. Marshall?"

"A teaspoon of both, thank you." Regina took the cup offered as her attention fell on two small children holding hands, in a frame sitting on the doctor's desk. She started to reach for it but quickly pulled her hand back. "May I?"

"Yes, please. These are my twins, Donni and Ronnie, at the age of five and a-half." Doctor Williams sipped on the hot coffee. "They take after their dear mother."

"They are so cute, just a little younger than my little girl. She is six." Regina returned the photo back to its rightful place.

"They are a little older now Regina. That picture was taken six and a half years ago." Todd Williams reached behind him and got a resent photo of his twins. "The boys are twelve now, almost teenagers. Joyce and I had them late in our life. I guess you might say, they help keep us young." He laughed and Regina noticed he was even more handsome when he laughed. The buzzer went off on the telephone and Doctor Williams picked up the receiver. "One moment please." He stood up and smiled down at the pretty blonde across from him.

"Excuse me Regina, I must take this call. Feel free to look around my office. I have a lot of interesting books, prints and antiques sitting over there. They may be of some interest until I return." The doctor took the phone into a small room connected to his office and shut the door.

Regina got up to stretch her legs and looked around. True to his words, Doctor Williams had many interesting objects lining his bookshelves. She was about to go and sit back down when a framed newspaper clipping caught her eye. Headlines written boldly across the front page of a six-and a half year old paper, read: LOCAL MAN GIVES HIS LIFE SO OTHERS MAY LIVE. Regina's heart melted as she re-read the same write up she had saved about her Michael and the faithful day he had saved two small children from certain death, knowing it meant receiving his own death. She bent in closer to read the names of the children. She had not remembered until now why the boys in the photo looked so familiar to her. Regina read the words softly to herself.

"Donnie and Ronnie Williams were thrown bravely into the arms of men Michael Marshall had pulled along with him as he ran to save the two children from being executed on live wires waiting under them as they clung, frighten and helpless, on a weak tree limb." Tears ran down Regina's face as she gazed into Michael loving eyes. She had not noticed Doctor Williams walking up beside her until he spoke softly.

"You have a good heart Regina. I will never forget that day and the sacrifice that young man gave to save my children. I know he is with the Lord."

"Yes, he is. Michael was like that Doctor Williams. He was the bravest, most given person I have ever known." Regina excepted the handkerchief the doctor offered her.

"You knew him?" he thought for a moment as his eyes fell on her. "Of course, you share the same last name. Is he a relative Regina? How are you kin to Michael?"

"Michael…is my husband, the father of Joby, my little girl, who was only five-months-old inside me when he gave his life." She sniffed. "Michael never got to see his little girl, at least alive."

"Regina." The gentleman put his arm around her for comfort. "Please, forgive me, I had no way of knowing you were married to my hero. After Jesus, Michael Marshall is the next person I want to see when I cross over into heaven." Todd took a deep breath, as he looked thoughtful. "Even before I see my dear wife, Joyce, who passed away two years ago from cancer."

"I'm truly sorry for your loss, Doctor Williams." Regina regained control over her emotions after hearing the good man speak such kind words about the man she would always love. "I guess you know then what it's like raising your children alone?"

"Please Regina, call me Todd. We are like a big family here at Mercy." He took her back to the chair and smiled down. "This is a Christian base hospital and my staff and I would love for you to become a part of our family."

"That sounds wonderful. So, how does this work Doc...Todd? Do I first attend the nursing academia for my degree, then come here to work?" Regina knew this man was true to his faith and in her heart, she knew working here beside him and the supporting staff of workers, would be a dream come true.

"You will take your training right here, at Mercy. We have a terrific group of teachers in our personal classrooms and the training you receive from each and your interactions with the patients, under supervision, is the best means of study. Hands on, Regina!" he smiled with confidence "I have a good eye of what to look for in a nurse. Her heart is always in her job and she, truly cares about her patients."

"Thank you for your vote of confidence, Todd." Regina returned his smile. "When do I start?"

"Tomorrow soon enough?" Todd stood up laughing. "I have a hunch if I had said today, your answer would have been yes!"

"And you would have been correct sir." Regina stood up and gathered her things. "Thank you for giving me my dream, Todd."

"You will make a great addition to our team, Regina. See you at seven a.m." the doctor walked her to the receptionist desk.

"Bright and early to learn." Regina let Todd help with her coat.

"Terrific! Now go tell your father and that darling little Joby, your good news." Todd watched her thank his secretary, for the coffee before she walked out and closed the door behind her. The doctor turned and walked back inside his office to his desk, then picked up her letter.

"What is it about that woman? Was it the fact that she was Michael Marshall's wife, his hero, his twin son's hero? He had not had this feeling since he met Joyce." He glanced in his mirror at himself. "Could I be falling in love? Could she love a man in his fifties or am I just being foolish?" Todd stepped closer to the mirror. He had missed two hair cut appointments and his hair hung over his ears, making him look younger. "I think I'll cancel my hair cut again. This style seems to suit my feelings." Smiling, Todd Williams picked up the phone to call Maglen Barber Shop.

Regina drove her car into her driveway, her mind on Todd Williams. He had mentioned he and his wife, Joyce, were both older when they had their sons, but Todd looked extremely handsome to her and she thought his hair was quite distinguish the way he wore it. When Todd had took around her to show comfort, Regina remembered having an incredible feeling flow through her body, much like it felt when Michael hugged her. Could she be falling in love with Todd, a man she barely knew?"

The telephone was ringing when she reached the front door. She answered it quickly before the answer machine picked it up.

"Regina, this is Todd." Again, the same warm feelings invaded her body, just from the sound of his voice. "I hope I haven't caught you at a bad time. I want be long."

"It's quite alright Todd. I just this minute walked in the door." She smiled to herself. "Did I forget something?"

"No, I did." Doctor Williams looked around the empty

office to make sure he was still alone. "There are two reasons for my call, Regina. First, I forgot to mention our dress code. We supply all staff members with a white jacket. What you wear under it, is up to you."

"That sounds easy enough." Regina felt relieved she did not have to wear a starched uniform. "What was your second reason for calling, Todd?" she was sure it would have something to do about work.

"Would you…" he swallowed. "Would you have dinner with me Saturday evening?" he waited nervously, hoping he had not overstepped his boundary.

"Yes Todd, I would love to have dinner with you." Regina closed her eyes in total surprise. Todd's heart was racing when he said happily.

"Wonderful! I will pick you up at 6:30. I was hoping you would say yes, so I made reservations at that French Restaurant on Fifth and Vine. The food is excellent and the mothers to be can choose from a fine selection of non-acholic wines, teas or coffees."

"It sounds perfect Todd and will give us a chance to learn more about one another." She checked her watch, hating to end the call. "Todd, I'm sorry to cut our call short, but Joby gets out of school soon and I don't want her to wait for me to come. I like to be there when she comes out."

Todd smiled, feeling good about this loving person. "You are a good mother Regina. Then you run on and I will look forward to seeing you in the morning." After they both said goodbye, the phone went silent and Regina grabbed her keys and purse, then raced back out the door, feeling a new sense of happiness.

Chapter 21

It had been a long day for Doctor Janet Shields in the delivery room at Maglen Hospital. She not only delivered two of her patient's babies, but had assisted with a third delivery. Three little boys, born very close to each other, each one with black hair and green eyes, much like her own Matthew.

Janet peeked in on her sleeping angel when she got home from her long rounds at the hospital. She had been happy with her choice of nanny for her young son, overruling Eric's choice, a much younger woman, blonde, well-figured and no experience when it came to watching a small child. Miss Fletcher came highly recommended, was more mature, middle age and a Christian woman who was perfect for her little Matthew. She walked into the den and dropped down into her favorite chair and excepted the glass of wine from her husband who smiled up from his paper.

"Looking in on Matt? You look tired Janet, busy day?"

"Three babies, born within hours of each other." She kicked her shoes off and took a sip of the rich red wine. "All three healthy, handsome little boys."

"All babies look the same to me." Eric laughed softly. "I guess they were triplets, correct?"

"They could have been. Their similarities were amazing." Janet closed her tired eyes and the precious little faces came into her mind. "Three different mothers."

"Just a coincidence, Janet." He laughed again and took a drink of his wine. "It only proves my point, all babies looked alike when they're born."

"Look Eric, I have delivered my share of babies over the years and there are no two baby that look alike, except these three." She opened her eyes and looked over at her husband. "Eric, I can still see our Matthew when he was born and he looked exactly like these three boys."

Eric looked up at her seriously. "Janet, what are you trying to say? Are you accusing me of having something to do with these three women getting pregnant?"

"That would mean you would have had an affair with all three women." She slipped her shoes back on her feet. "And at the same time."

"Janet, this is ridicules!" Eric slammed down his paper. "I thought you trusted me! I have never had an affair with one woman, much less three!"

"Calm down Eric, I am not accusing you." Janet got up and took her glass to the stairs, then turned to face him "By the way dear, all three mothers had blonde hair, natural blondes, and blue eyes. Amazing all three boys had black hair and green eyes." She walked up to her bedroom as Eric watched her closely. Nervously, he drank down his wine and retreated to the kitchen for another glass before turning in.

The years passed quickly and all four boys grew into fine young men, attending colleges such as Harvard, Yale, and Princeton. Each had won free scholarships for their outstanding grades.

Rebecca and Zechariah's son, Joshua Benjamin, became a Doctor of Religion and with his outreach sermons, he became a sought-after evangelist and faith healer. Whether on television or big seated coliseums, football stadiums or great cathedrals, wherever you could seat a large group of people, his banner flew boldly behind him stating: "JOSHUA FIGHTS THE BATTLE OF LUCIFER AND SIN COMES TUMBLING DOWN!"

Victoria and Eli Spilman's son Steven, became a highly skilled scientist who was working in a renowned lab, discovering cures for various diseases and unknown virus'. His reputation spread throughout the states in a short period of time. Steven was highly sought after for his God given talent.

Regina and Todd Williams' son, Michael, found his God given talent in his expert skills as a surgeon. His long steady fingers could perform the most delicate operation, where one slip could mean instant death. Michael Marshall Williams never lost a single patient. As with Joshua Benjamin and Steven Spilman, Michael was highly sought after for his unique calmness and the fact that he would always say a prayer before he began his operations. Michael could always feel a sense of peace fall on his patients and a warm feeling would ingulf him before he began. The young surgeon would never take the credit for saving his patients, He gave the glory to his God, The God who gave this young man of faith, the peace that passes all understanding.

Matthew Shields followed in his mother's steps and became a doctor and a heart surgeon and just like her, he spread his medical skills throughout the entire hospital. It was here where Matthew got the call that would change the small town of Maglen forever. A rare virus was spreading throughout the United States. At the present time, there was no known cure for the deadly disease. The man over the phone was completely serious as he spoke to the young doctor.

"The Federal Government has discovered an undercover operation, set up in America, by a foreign militant group. They have recruited hundreds of women volunteers to work in brothels and prostitute houses in both the big towns as well as small towns. Anywhere to bring out their objective and that is to destroy as many American lives as possible. These select group of women have pledged to be martyrs for the cause. Each woman was injected with the deadly virus to spread to unsuspecting clients.

The disease will be spread when passed on to anyone the client has had sex with. It is highly contagious and easily spread. The effects come sift and the window for survival are very small if at all. If a cure is not found immediately, thousands of our citizens will die." The phone fell silent for a moment as Matthew heard the caller take a deep breath, indicating more bad news.

"Doctor Shields, we hate to inform you that your small town of Maglen is on their hit list. One Sadie's Ladies, hired a militant prostitute, blonde, blue eyed, beautiful and very deadly to anyone who received her services. Her name is Paris Evans and her real name is Zuma Pichai, age twenty-five, died one month after arriving in Maglen, but not until she infected twenty men, some local, others from neighboring towns. Anyone who has come in contact with this woman is urged to seek medical help immediately. This information has been passed on to your local paper and news stations.

My prayers are with you Doctor Shields. If you need to speak to me Matthew, this is Michael Marshall Williams.

Chapter 22

Eric had read through the article three times. Sweat ran down his face as he could visualize the beautiful blonde with the French accent. Paris Evans, so young, so alive, so sexy. He threw the newspaper across the room then grabbed his trembling lips. "So deadly, the little bitch!"

Janet had walked in time to witness her husband throw the paper angrily and make his angry remark.

"Eric, are you alright? Why did you throw the newspaper across the den and stop yelling before you strain your vocal cords?"

"My vocal cords?" he laughed sarcastically. "I am so stupid!"

"Eric, please calm down and tell why you are so upset." She walked over by his side, looking down with concern. She noticed his brow was dripping. "Eric, you are sweating terribly darling, don't you feel well?"

"Janet, I...I could be dying!" he blurted out.

"What?" Janet quickly checked his chest to see if his heart was beating normal. "Eric, does your chest hurt? The way you're sweating, you could be having a heart attack."

"I wish I were!" tears filled his green eyes as he looked up at his devoted wife. "The sad thing is, you could be dying too Janet and it's all my fault!"

"Me? Dying?" Janet eyes fell on the paper he had thrown. She walked over and picked it up, reading the headlines. "Prostitute Dies! Link With, a Militant Group to Wipe Out Thousands!" Janet stared down at the words as she remembered Matthew telling her and the staff about Michael Benjamin calling and he gave the group the full report. Janet remembered feeling sorry for all the innocent wives whose husbands did business with Sadie's Ladies. Now, she wondered if she could be one of those statistics. She walked back over to her husband and held the paper up in defiance. "God, Eric, are you telling me, you have been paying prostitutes for sex?"

"Janet, I…" Eric Shields broke down. "I'm sorry Janet. I don't know what is wrong with me, but I eat and breathe sex. My body…I require sex every night. I could not ask you, your work…I.."

"Eric, why in the name of God didn't you get help for your sex craving? You wouldn't be the first person who has it!" Janet was understandably upset. "I'm a doctor, you could have come to me."

"I enjoyed sex too much to give it up and now…" he fell back in his chair crying. "I have infected Brook! How do I tell her? She gave up 'everything' for me!"

"Brook? Brook Falls?" Janet felt sick. "You don't have to tell her Eric, she already knows. Brook Falls came into the hospital today for a checkup after hearing the news on the television. She was afraid she might have contracted this fatal virus!" Eric jumped out of his chair and grabbed his wife as tears fell from his eyes.

"No! Not Brook!"

Janet had never seen emotion like this from Eric, not ever.

"Eric, do you love this Brook? Be honest with me?" she spoke softly.

"I'm sorry Janet. I have always loved you, in my own way. We are good partners together." Eric looked down at her, his voice trembling. "But, I love Brook Falls more than I thought possible. She knows me, Janet. She knows my faults and my weaknesses, and yet, this beautiful person excepts me for what I am and she loves me totally and completely."

"I can understand why you find yourself hard to love, Eric. You have always been self-righteous and thought only of yourself." Janet felt a headache coming on as Eric fell back in his chair and dropped his head. "Besides this Brook, whom you love, and this Militant, Zuma Pichai, how many others have there been Eric, and do not lie to me!"

"Remember when you had three women who had three babies delivered near each other and all three sons resembled me?" Eric swallowed nervously as he confessed. "They could have been mine, two I know for sure."

"Eric, you told me you did not have an affair with those three women!" Janet almost shouted and was glad they were alone in the big house. "Another lie?"

"No Janet, it was not a lie.' Eric stood up and walked over to looked out at the growing darkness. He did not want to look his wife in the eyes when he made his confession. "I did have an affair with two of those women, but I raped the younger woman."

"Eric Shields! Could you not get enough willing women to have sex with?" Janet threw the paper at him as tears streamed down her face. "God, Eric, you could ruin an innocent girl's entire life! Why?"

"I was obsessed with Rebecca! She was out of my reach! The God she believed in kept her away from me!" he turned to face her, eyes blazing. "I had to have her, feel her young body next to mine."

"And were you with your devoted Brook at that time, Eric?" Janet threw the girl he confessed to love, up in his face.

"Yes Janet, Brook and I have been together ever since she started to college. Brook helped me get her cousin. She would do anything for me. Her devotion goes beyond the boundaries and her love for me is endless." Eric spoke loudly. "Now Brook may be dying and it's all my fault."

"Yes Eric, your sickness has affected many women! Not necessarily with this deadly virus, but you took away a little bit of each woman you had sex with!" Janet walked over to the stairs "make an appointment first thing in the morning, then pack your things and get out!"

"Janet, please, you have got to forgive me!" Eric begged. "Where will I go?"

"To Brook, if she will still have you!" Janet closed her eyes to hold in her tears "I still have my work, if I survive. If not, I know I will live on in heaven." Her eyes fell sadly on her husband. "I feel sorry for you Eric! Where is your hope?"

"Hope? Are you referring to this make-believe God, Janet?" he felt sick.

"Eric, don't some small part of you hope for life after death?" Janet genuinely felt sad for Eric. "You may not be aware of this, but you will have a life after death, only yours will sadly be in hell if you do not change now." Janet watched his face, waiting for his usual sneer. It didn't come. "Eric, for the first time since I've known you, I can see there may still be a chance for you to turn your life around. I must admit, I give the credit to Brook Falls."

"Brook? Why Janet?" Eric saw only love in her eyes now. The hatred had melted away.

"Brook has given you a special kind of love and I can see you love her just as deeply." Janet walked over and touched his tear-stain face "Love comes from God, Eric, and somewhere deep inside Brook is the belief in God, perhaps hiding her faith from you for your love and approval. Weather you can see it or not, Brook has touched your cold heart and placed warm love inside, dear Eric."

"Janet, you are a good woman and I will always care about you." Eric could hardly speak, his emotions torn between two women he loved. "You will forgive me, please darling?"

"I am a Christian, Eric. Forgiveness lives in my heart, so yes, I forgive you." Janet reached up and kissed him. "I sincerely pray we all get good reports in the morning, but if we get the worst, I will pray for God's healing for all of us."

"Thank you, Janet. I never really deserved you." Eric held her hand lovingly. "I must admit, I'm very proud of our son, Matt."

"Our son is a great doctor, but most important, he is a good Christian man, despite his father's attempt to make him see things his way." She gently touched his face when he smiled. "Eric, you love Brook. She is the one you need to spend the rest of your life with, no matter how long or God forbid, how short. Matt and I will always be here for you." Janet took his shaking hand and pulled him up the steps. "Now try and get some rest. Tomorrow we will find out if we are infected or in the clear."

Eric followed Janet up to the bedrooms, but this night they slept wrapped in each other's arms.

Chapter 23

"Dad, I am truly sorry, but you have the deadly virus and it appears to be spreading quickly." Eric and Janet Shields had sat down with their son Matthew when they first arrived at Maglen Hospital for test. They told him all about his father's past. It took a while for Matthew to process all the sordid information, but after turning it over in his head, he knew time did not allow for him to hold hard feelings for the man who had shown him very little love throughout his life. So, Matthew simply forgave his father so he could move forward with the test.

Both Brook and Janet had also been infected and had been given similar diagnosis. They were admitted to the third floor for observation. Then the word came to Doctor Shields informing him that a cure had been found by Doctor Steven Spilman, the renowned scientist and he was personally on his way to Maglen, along with the highly skilled surgeon, Michael Marshall Williams.

"Doctor Spilman, Doctor Williams, it is an honor to meet you both again." Matthew Shields shook their hand. "It has been a long time since we were in grade school. We are truly humbled that you chose our small town to personally come and help us." Matthew noticed their attention was on the patients resting in the big room in front of them as he continued.

"I am sure you have a great many good teams going to every city and town that have been hit but I cannot imagine why you both chose the small town of Maglen."

"As you stated Matthew, Maglen was our hometown and Doctor Janet Shields, your dear mother, brought us into this world." Michael smiled. "When we read she was among the ones infected, there was no question as to where we would go."

"So, my mother delivered you both, right here at Maglen Hospital." Matthew could not get over how much these two important gentlemen resembled him.

Both doctors had been observing the patients from the hall window when they felt Doctor Shields observing them closely. "Matthew, I cannot help but notice how you are staring at us. Do we seem to be a carbon copy of each other, and yes, you, as well?" Steven bent in close, "There is a reason we look alike, Matthew. We two are your half-brothers. The other brother has just arrived in town to have a special healing crusade tonight at Maglen University. Maybe you remember him, Evangelist Joshua Benjamin."

"Joshua Benjamin! I have watched him many times on television. His powerful words reach out to overwhelming-audiences." Matthew had mixed emotions, learning he had not one, but three half- brothers, all important in their own field. These three men had to be the boys his mother and father had told him about earlier. He wondered which one was from the young girl his father had raped. Ironically, now they were here to help the very man that had rejected them and walked out on each of their mothers because they had refused to have them aborted.

"I know this must be hard for you to take in Matthew, all at once." Michael touched his brother's shoulders for the first time. "Especially with your father and mother fighting for their life."

"The 'sins' of 'our' father has finally caught up with him and he is bringing mom and his true love, Brook Falls, down with him." Matthew had tears in his eyes and he felt only love and respect for his newly found brothers. "I know it cannot come easy for you to help Eric, with the way he treated your mothers and rejecting you, but it gives me the peace of mind to have you by my side. I won't have to go down this road alone now."

114

"This Eric, merely planted the seed in my mother, my brother, but with the extra love given by our dear mothers and fathers, we have grown in the Christian faith and take our professions strongly. All patients are the same in our eyes and we treat them equally and strive for success."

Matthew had brought both specialist into room 306 and would give out instructions.

"Each of you will be taken into the operation room, one at a time. Doctor Williams will perform the operations with me to assist him, while Doctor Spilman prepares the correct dose of the drug to be administered safely into a small incision."

"This is where the operation can be tricky. Once the incision is made, the drug must be placed quickly and with a steady hand." Doctor Spilman continued. "One wrong slip and this drug goes directly into the blood stream, and that can be fatal. My friends, you are in the best possible hands with Doctor Michael Williams. He is the top in his field."

"There are three of you. Brook and Eric have the worse cases, so I suggest we take Brook first, then Eric, then Janet." Michael looked around at the small group and noticed Eric's hand go up. "Yes, Professor Shields?"

"Brook first, then Janet and I will go last." His voice was steady. "Please, Doctor Williams, the ladies must go ahead of me. If anyone dies, let it be me."

"Eric?" Brook reached out to touch his fingers he held out for her weak hand.

"Eric, please." Janet was cut off by her son as he looked down at his father.

"Dad, it does my heart good to know you are finally putting someone before yourself."

"It is the right thing to do, Matt. I feel it." Eric closed his eyes, sadness gripping him as he watched the two women he loved sick and possibly dying. "Besides, I'm probably to mean to die."

"We will have no such talk, Mr. Shields." Steven waved the staff of workers to take Brook into the operation room. She looked one last time at the man she loved and adored as her lips moved the words, 'I love you.' Through sudden tears, Eric said softly,

"I love you too Brook."

Steven watched Janet's expression and only found love radiating off her beautiful face. He cleared his throat. "We will not stop until all three of you are given the drug." With that the group left to begin on Brook.

Coming in an hour later, they rolled Janet out, telling Eric Brook had been taken to the recovery room so he wouldn't worry about her not returning. When they had finished with Janet, they left her outside in the hall so Eric would not see her. They came and got him and rolled him out another door.

When Eric opened his drowsy eyes, he looked around the room, Janet smiled weakly from the bed on his right. Turning to see Brook in the bed on his left side, he only saw a made-up bed. Eric remembered her lying there beside him, too weak to talk much, Eric sit straight up and looked nervously around, then back at his wife.

"Janet, where did they take Brook? She is not in her bed! It's been made up!" Eric noticed Janet's eyes were sad with possible bad news. "Janet?"

"They put her in a private room, Eric. They could not operate on Brook."

"Not operate? But...why?" he felt sudden panic. Without the operation she had no hope in pulling through. "I don't understand."

"It was her heart Eric. The deadly virus had spread to Brook's heart and lungs. To make the incision would have meant instant death for her. They wanted Brook to have time to say...goodbye, my darling."

"God! Janet, no!" Eric tried to climb from the bed but fell back down, too weak to get up. "Why? Why wasn't it me instead of my perfect angel. Brook does not deserve to die! God, what have I done to my Brook?" he cried.

"Father!" Matthew noticed his father trying to get out of bed, "You must stay in bed and rest."

"Son, I beg you, take me to Brook! I must see her one last time before..." Eric Shields broke down sobbing.

Feeling compassion for his father, Matthew rolled a wheelchair up by his bed and help him in the seat.

"I will take you to see her so you can tell her goodbye." Matthew found it hard to speak. "She has been calling out for you."

"Thank you, son, thank you." Eric squeezed Matthew's arm lovingly and for the first time in the young man life, Matthew felt a small amount of love from his father.

Matthew left the room and shut the door as Eric lifted himself up beside of Brook's bedside. She lay peacefully sleeping, as if she had fallen asleep after making love to him, as she had often done. Tears once again filled his green eyes as he looked down at her angelic face,

"Why Brook, why did this have to happen to my girl? My friend, my...my only love." Eric heard voices just outside the door. Quickly he sat back down in the wheelchair and rolled behind the curtain to hide himself from the visitor.

The door opened slowly and closed quietly as light footsteps moved to Brook's bed. The sound of a chair being pulled up next to Brook and then only silence.

Chapter 24

Then Eric heard it, the voice of an angel, singing so sweet and clear and a song meant just for his Brook.

"Jesus loves you, Brook, I know. For the Bible tells me so. Little ones to Him belong, you are weak but He is strong. Yes, Jesus loves you, Yes, Brook, He loves you. Yes, Jesus loves you, because He told me so!"

"Rebecca!" Brook smiled and opened her tired eyes. "I thought...I was hearing an angel from heaven and that God had forgiven me."

"God has never stopped loving you, Brook." Rebecca took her cousin's frail hand. "There is no sin, no matter how great, that cannot be forgiven."

"Then...I must ask you, my favorite cousin and dearest friend, to...forgive me." Tears flooded from her eyes. "I was so blind by Eric's love, I would do anything for him. Even betray our friendship."

"Then it was you who told Eric all about me and the men in my life, including my own daddy." Rebecca's voice remained sweet and calm. "I have had my suspicions for years, Brook, Then, one day, I spotted Eric coming out of your apartment and I saw how you were holding on to him in your farewell kiss. There was no doubt who had raped me after my son was born and he looked just like Eric."

"You never confronted me if you thought I was involved in what happened. Nor did you bring charges up against Eric for raping you. Why Rebecca?" Brook's heart was hurting and only partly from the virus pain. "I never meant to hurt you."

"I know love can make you do foolish things Brook," Rebecca rubbed her cousin's hot forehead with a cool rag. "Of course, I forgive you Brook. Now you only need to ask God to forgive you for your adultery with a married man and mostly for denying our Savior and Lord, just to please Eric."

"You know? Then you must know I have always loved the Lord in my heart, Rebecca. I could never stop loving the one who saved me from all my sin. I did it for Eric, I love him so and he was so strong in his unbelief, I didn't want to lose him or his love." She cried. "Now, I don't want to die and go to hell because of my denial or my adultery. Rebecca, I want to go to heaven, to see my mama and daddy, to see Jesus. But Rebecca, if I go to heaven…I will never see my true love, ever again!" she started crying.

"If Eric don't change and believe in our Lord, his memory will be erased from your mind after you go to heaven, sweet girl." Rebecca saw hurt in Brook's eyes. "But Brook, there's always hope, Eric might see the light and learn to believe. I will certainly pray for him. I do not wish to see any of God's children lost to Satan."

"Please help him when I'm gone, Rebecca. Help him learn to believe and see the truth. I wish I had the time to help my darling, but my time is limited." Brook tried to smile. "You seem very happy cousin. Your marriage must be good."

"Better than good, Brook. Zechariah and I travel with our son on his evangelist crusades. Zech and Joshua preach, and I sing the glories of God's perfect love." Rebecca noticed the wheels behind the curtain move and realized someone had been listening to their conversation from a wheelchair. Suddenly it dawned on her that it must be Eric. She knew he really loved Brook and thought, it was time to heal.

"Brook, it was a bad thing Eric did to me, but something very important and wonderful came out of it."

Rebecca turned to the person waiting just outside the open door and motioned him in. "The rape brought forth a son and he became a special gift from God." Rebecca smiled at the handsome young man as he took her hand and smiled down at Brook. "Brook, this is my son, Joshua Benjamin."

"Joshua Benjamin, the young evangelist! I have watched

you on television and witness all those people who have been saved or healed by your loving words." Brook seem to glow when she gazed up at the man who resembled her Eric. "Tell me Joshua, will I see Jesus today?"

"Sweet Brook, child of God, do you repent of your sins and ask the Lord Jesus to forgive you and take you into His glory?"

"Oh, yes! Yes, I do!" she smiled. "Sweet Lord, forgive me of all my many sins and renew me in your loving bosom."

"You shall be with the Savior very soon, sister Brook." Joshua held her hand as he spoke softly. "Please come out Eric and tell Brook what is in your heart before she goes to her eternal home."

Eric closed his eyes and rolled out on the other side of the woman he loved so much. Brook reached for his hand and smiled.

"Eric, have you been there the whole time, my darling? You need your rest."

"I needed to see you, my dearest Brook." Eric could not control his tears as he held on to her hand tightly. "Brook, I have loved you for a very long time, and only you, darling. How can I let you go when I need you so much?"

"Eric darling, never blame yourself for what has happened to me, I do not blame you." Tears filled her beautiful eyes. "Yes, you gave us the virus that has threatened our lives, but it was my weak heart, a family trait, that caused the virus to invade it so quickly and cut my life short." Brook squeezed his hand. "It is so hard to leave you Eric, my deepest love, especially knowing how you feel about faith in God."

"Brook, I should have never asked you to give up your faith just because I did not believe in this God you love." Eric could not bear watching her suffer with each breath. "My darling, when you ask me if you could let your hair go natural, it was easy for me to say yes, because I love you so much. I never told you this, but Brook, you look even more beautiful with your black hair, flowing long over your shoulders."

"Sweet, my darling, the one thing that would have made me happy, would have been if I could have been your one and only love. If I could have become Mrs. Eric Shields." Brook felt his face, knowing soon she might never see him ever again, Tears flooded her vision as she said softly. "Eric, will you promise me something? It is my dying wish, my love."

"Anything Brook. I will do anything you ask of me, I promise." Eric Shields' heart was breaking.

"Your son Joshua, is holding a healing crusade tonight at the university. I want you to go Eric. Please darling, just go and listen to him. Don't go with a negative attitude but with an open heart." Brook took a labored breath. "Eric, my love, I want to see you in heaven! To forget you ever existed would be hard for you. Promise me…you will go."

Eric looked up into his son's eyes and saw only love and compassion.

"Eric, tell her sir, while there's time. They are coming for her, to take her home. I can smell heaven's veil opening up." Joshua spoke with passion as he looked down at the dying young woman. "The angels have arrived, my beautiful sister. There will be no more pain, only great love and complete joy."

Brook looked up into Eric's tear-stain green eyes, a heavenly glow around her head.

"Eric, I see the angels. Please, my darling, say your last words to me."

"Brook, my heart will always belong to you. I love you so very much." He wept as he said. "I will go tonight, my darling, I promise. I will listen with an opened heart. I cannot stand the thought of never seeing your beautiful smiling face again nor can I live with the knowledge of you not remembering me or how much you loved me." Eric watched her smile into his eyes then slowly looked up, her radiance getting brighter.

"Brook?" Eric bent down close to her and whispered "Brook, my love?"

Brook smiled up at him, a peaceful glow on her beautiful face, then she touched his mouth loving as she said softly "Kiss me Eric."

His lips parted over the lips of the girl he loved for the last time as she took her last breath.

Chapter 25

Eric Shields lay in his hospital bed watching the evening news with Victoria Spilman. His heart was torn with grief at the lost of Brook. Life as he knew it would never be the same. His promise to attend the big crusade would be kept. It was his Brook's dying wish and he would honor it.

Eric watched as Victoria looked out solemn into the camera and spoke from her heart.

"A great tragedy has hit our small town and effected a great many of our fine citizens. So far there have been seven deaths linked to the Verta Virus, a highly contagious disease that has been passed on to some customers at Sadie's Ladies, thought to have been an escort service for gentlemen. The owner, Sadie Warren, has been under investigation for some time. She called in to report the death of one of her new escorts, Paris Evans, twenty-five- years of age. It was at this time Mrs. Warren tearfully confessed to running a house of prostitution for more than thirty years and up until Miss Evans came, things ran smooth. Mrs. Warren said she kept a clean group of women whose only goal was to keep the customers satisfied and make a good salary.

As you have read by now in the Maglen Journal, Miss Evans real name was Zuma Pichai, a foreign militant whose orders were to come to our town, seek out a list of names provided and destroy. As of this hour, there are only two victims remaining in Maglen Hospital, waiting for the new-found cure to work. The third victim, Brook Falls, passed away this morning at the age of 44, a young lady who contracted the virus through her love interest who was a victim of Zuma Pichai.

We are asking that everyone out there in Maglen and surrounding towns in our viewing area, to pray for Professor

Eric Shields and his lovely wife, Janet Shields. We hope to see everyone tonight at Maglen University for the healing crusade with Doctor Joshua Benjamin. This is Victoria Sinclair Spilman, whose heart is full of hope and faith that Eric and Janet are both healed tonight. Goodnight and God bless each one."

"Just how many men and their love ones did that bitch kill?" Eric hated the militant for taking his Brook from him.

"Calm down Eric, it's not good to get so upset. It could raise your blood pressure." Janet reached over and took his trembling hand and noticed it felt ice cold. "Eric, you are freezing! I will ring for a nurse."

"Just let me die, Janet! I don't want to live without Brook!" Eric cried. "I have nothing left to live for."

"Eric, that is where you are wrong." Regina walked in with a warming pad and wool blanket and wrapped him up. "You have a very forgiving wife and a son who has always needed his father."

Recognizing her, Eric choked back his tears as she took his blood pressure. He said her name softly "Regina."

"Although you have four sons Eric, all special gifts from God, Father Zechariah Benjamin, spoke to three scared women when we were faced with our difficult decisions, whether or not to have an abortion or choose life for our innocent babies."

"Regina, you were always a special woman. I can see that you are a caring nurse as well as a wise councilor." Eric gave her a weak smile.

"You are right, Professor Shields. My loving wife is both a terrific nurse whose love and care for all her patients led her in to becoming a councilor to those patients facing troubles or worries." Doctor Todd Williams had walked up beside his wife. Regina had told Todd all about her love affair with Eric, even though it was a business arrangement and it was through that relationship, she had gotten pregnant with Michael, the second. "Regina is the best at doing both and if you wish to get any better, Mr. Shields, I suggest you listen to her."

"There is really nothing worth saving, Doctor Williams. I'm not worth her help. She should hate me for walking out on her without even a decent goodbye." Eric closed his eyes in despair. "I just want to die, go into the emptiness of death and forget all about everything I lost. My Brook is dead and I will never see her again!"

"If you die soon Eric, you will not go into a black empty place forever, forever gone, forever forgotten, over time. The way you believe now Eric, you probably would have wished for that empty place that exist only in your mind. Whether or not you believe me Eric, the fact is true, you will go to a place far worse, unless you change."

"You speak of this…hell, you believe exist?" he forced a smile. "Maybe I deserve it then, Regina."

"Eric, no matter what you have done, and it has been plenty, no one wishes for you to spend your eternity in hell, especially your Brook." Regina watched as Eric turned to face her, questions filling his green eyes. "Brook is not dead Eric. Brook has merely moved from this world, through the invisible veil, to her eternal home."

"Regina is right Eric. That is why Brook wanted you to go tonight." Janet had tears in her eyes when Eric looked at her. She could not see the sneer he usually got whenever someone spoke of their faith, it was not on his face, only uncertainty. "Brook wants to see you again, Eric darling. She truly loves you. I could see it, feel it." Janet's lips formed a sweet smile as she reached over and touched his hand, "I must admit, your Brook was more devoted to you than I ever was." She noticed his uncertainty only grew with that confession. "It's not what you're thinking Eric. I have always been faithful to you and our marriage. I was referring to my job. My work is my passion, so I admit the hospital and my medical practice always came first, even before you, my darling. I can see how

125

you fell in love with Brook. She is truly a warm loving young lady who has always gave her best to the man she loved and adored, you Eric."

"Janet, you speak about Brook as though she were present, alive?" Eric's eyes were pale, but there was a smile upon his lips.

"Yes Eric, we have told you Brook is very much alive and she could be watching you right now while she stands beside her Savior. Praying that the man she loves will go and listen to what your son Joshua has to say tonight and..." Regina felt his hot forehead. "and heal your body and soul."

Eric could see concern on Regina's face as she filled in his chart. He gently touched her hand.

"I'm getting worse, aren't I? I must at least hold out for tonight. I promise Brook I would be there."

"Eric, what happen to you as a child?" Regina wanted to take his mind off dying and understand why he did not believe in God. "You spoke of your mother often when we were together. You must have loved her dearly."

"The woman I was speaking about was like a mother to me and I loved her dearly. She was not the wretched woman who bore me, despised me, as did my father!" Eric's look was far away as he continued. "I did not realize how they felt about me until the Sunday we returned from church."

"So, as a young boy, you attended church." Regina's voice was soft and tender. "Did you believe in Jesus when you were a small boy?"

"At six-years-old, I was easy to empress into believing in fairy tales." His eyes met Regina's, expecting aggravation but he only found understanding and love.

"A child can receive faith from a true and pure heart, Eric. Believe me when I say, your child-like faith was very real but something happened to cause you to turn away. Tell us Eric, what happen to you that makes you feel the way you do?"

"I had a very loving and kind Sunday school teacher, Mrs.

126

Parks. I looked forward to attending her class on Sunday mornings. One Sunday she asked us to learn a Bible verse, any verse, by heart and recite it the following Sunday in class. She told us, if we could recite a verse, she would reward us with a gift and a gold star by our name. I studied all week and was happy that I had memorized the 23rd Psalm."

"The 23rd Psalm, at six-years-old? Wow! I bet Mrs. Parks was surprised you had chosen such a long passage in the Bible." Regina gave a genuine smile.

"Mrs. Parks was overjoyed. Mama and daddy, not so much." Eric closed his eyes as he remembered how happy he had been and excited to share the good news with his parents and was met with hate. "My teacher said I did extra good, so she placed four gold stars by my name. The joy I felt just looking at those sparkling gold stars by Eric Shields, was more than that six-year-old had ever felt. Then Mrs. Parks gave me my gift. A little white Bible of my very own. All the other children in my class, clapped for me. No one in the class got jealous and I must have inspired them, because they all promised our teacher they would learn a longer verse the next time. Especially Billy Baxter, whose verse was two little words, "He wept." Eric laughed softly remembering the chubby, red-hair and freckled boy who had got up and said the two words, then smiled proudly. Regina and Janet joined in his laughter, then stopped when Eric grew solemn.

"Mrs. Parks kissed my cheek and told me my parents would be so proud of me and that made me so happy, because that was the reason I had studied so hard, to make my parents proud of me. I tried to share my good news with them in the car going home from church, but their arguments between them never gave me the opportunity."

"Eric, did you ever get to tell your ungrateful parents what you had done?" Janet's heart was breaking for the man she loved.

"It was at the dining room table where we had sat down to

have a late lunch. Mama and daddy started eating as usual and I remember Mrs. Parks telling us to always say our blessing before we had our meal and again to pray at bedtime, thanking God for everything He had given us. As they talked to one another, I bowed my head and said a silent blessing. When I looked up, both my parents were staring at me." A tear ran down Eric's cheek as he thought back. "My father broke the stillness as he spoke loudly and said, "Eric, just what the hell are you doing?' Frightened by his stare, I answered softly, 'saying my prayer to thank God, sir'. My father just sneered and grew silent, so I got brave enough to speak up and told them about learning the Bible verse and how my teacher placed four gold stars by my name. Then I took out my white Bible and laid it on the table next to me. My mother reached across the table and placed it inside her pocket as she laughed and said it was a silly gift to give a six-year-old kid who could not understand one damn thing in the book! Then she kept it and drank down her wine and refilled her glass. I remember my little heart breaking because she had taken the one thing I wanted and had worked for. I remember trying to take my first bite as tears fell from my eyes and Mother reaching across the table to slap my head as she yelled at me that it was my daddy that provided the food we enjoyed, not God!"

"Eric, did your parents kill your belief in God?" Regina had pity for such a small child whose faith had been torn away by his own parents.

"I guess I tried to keep believing as long as we attended church. It happened slowly, my learning the truth. As I grew older, I learned my mother brought men in when father was out of town selling his wares. Later I found out she was a prostitute, getting paid by those men and father was in on it. I got home one day early from school and heard several voices making unusual sounds. I had walked in on an orgy. Both my parents along with three more couples from our church were taking turns on one another."

"Oh, my God, Eric! No child should have to witness that!" Janet could not believe anyone could be so brazen. "Did they catch you watching?"

"Oh yes and all hell broke loose! You would have thought that I was the one caught doing some sinful act! My 'wonderful' mother slapped my face while my loving father remained on Wanda Cummings and told me to get the hell out of his house and take nothing with me! He was in a rage, shouting, everything belongs to us, we paid for it! Then he said Get out and never come back!"

Eric closed his eyes, trying to blot out their faces. "I left that day, never to set my foot back inside that house. But, before leaving, I took every cent I could find. Not only from my parent's wallets, but all the other hypocrites. They tried to trace me down to get back their stolen money and have me thrown in to jail, hoping I would rot, but I covered my tracks. I only took what belonged to me, to get a new start. I was only fifteen."

"Fifteen? So, of course you dropped out of school." Regina took his hand. "Where did you go Eric?"

"I bought a bus ticket and took off across the country to look for a job. That is when I met the Myers, Bill and Betty. They took in a fifteen -year-old runaway and treated him like their own. They gave me an education because they saw potential in me. Bill and Betty owned a grocery store, nothing fancy but well stocked. I worked there for the first summer but they thought I was too smart to waste my time selling groceries so they took out a loan and sent me to college.

When Bill died almost thirty years ago, I took care of Betty and made sure she had the best care possible when she had to go into a nursing home." Eric turned to Janet. "I paid for all her bills Janet. Not just for pay back for everything they had given me but because I sincerely loved her. She was the mother I never had."

"Eric, they sounded like a good loving couple." Regina

thought a moment, then spoke "Did they never try to convince you to start going back to church and start believing again?"

Eric laughed, but this time it was not mocking, more like, I've got one on you, laugh. Sensing the tone of his laugh, Regina squinted her eyes and ask

"What exactly are you trying to tell us, Eric?"

"Bill and Betty were good loving people, Regina. You are correct about that. I've known them to give their last penny to a friend in need or someone hungry, free groceries."

"They sound like good Christians to me." Janet added.

"Then you would be mistaken, dear Janet. Bill and Betty told me that people needed to help each other because life was short and like the flowers, we all wither and die. The Myers were Atheist, ladies. They showed me where real love comes from, no matter how brief. It comes from every person born to man. Some people are born with love in their heart other only hate, like my parents."

"Eric, you have been twisted into two directions." Regina could understand why Eric felt there was no God. "First, your parents did you a misjustice by pretending to be Christians and going to church, probably for show or to find the right 'friends' to fit into their lifestyle. Their actions misguided you and then treating you like the heathens they really were. Then the Myers, who obviously treated you more like a son than you own parents, but did you a misjustice by feeding you with their beliefs in Atheism. The sad truth Eric is that both your unsuitable parents and the Myers fed you lies that hurt you."

"Brook told me, if I got to heaven, I would see her again. Would Bill and Betty be there too? They did good deeds all their life, for friends, for family, even for strangers."

"Eric, it is not our place to make judgement on anyone, but I believe in the words of God, the words of Jesus. I know there is no amount of good deeds we may do on our own that can save us without first believing in the Son of God." Regina looked deep within Eric's green serious eyes. "I believe if you give yourself to Jesus, believe in Him with all your heart and ask Him to forgive your sins, you will see Brook again when you pass from this world into the next." She gently squeezed his hand. "I also believe you will not find Bill or Betty there, unless they came to know the Lord, and unless your parents changed, you will not find them there either, nor will you remember them."

"But, if Jesus is filled with this incredible love and is so good, surely He would know how good they were." Eric could not wrap his head around those two- loving people being kept out of Heaven.

"You will get your answers tonight, Eric. Just listen with an open heart." Regina stood up and collected her things "The doctors will be in shortly with a report on your progress. I pray there is good new for both of you."

"I would think you would not care what happened to me Regina, after what I did to you." Eric felt chills and pulled the blanket around his neck.

"Eric, I wish you only the best as I do all my patients." Regina wrote something down on his chart, then smiled up at Eric and Janet. "Since all my children are grown and out on their own, I pour my time and energy into three places, first my Holy Family. Second, Todd, my wonderful husband, and then my nursing." Regina walked to the door. "As your nurse, I am asking both of you to rest quietly until the doctors arrive with your reports." She clicked the overhead light off and closed the door.

Chapter 26

Eric could not shake the scared feeling he had in his stomach after Doctor Williams and Doctor Spilman came in with their reports. Janet had been given a clean report. All her blood work had shown the operation was a total success and that all signs of the Verta Virus had completely been destroyed.

Eric's report did not fare as well. It would appear although the operation had gone well and the drug had been administered quickly and safely into the correct spot, some of the deadly virus had managed to get into his blood stream. After checking Eric's vital signs, they knew it was the virus causing his chills and was responsible for turning his skin pale and cold. Janet was scared for her husband and wanted him to be able to attend the service that night. Not just for Brook, but for herself and their son, Matthew. Mostly Janet wanted it for Eric himself, so he could hear the one who could help him heal both his body and soul.

"Is there nothing more you can do, Doctor Williams? Maybe if you place some of that drug into his veins, either by injection or through a dripping tube, it would kill the virus in his blood." Janet was holding out hope that this might be a solution to stop the spreading germ. Doctor Spilman looked down sadly at the woman who delivered him as a baby in this very hospital.

"The virus is too widely spread, Doctor Shields. I would love to tell you yes, it might work but this virus is too strong and it has already affected all his organs. We cannot give either of you false hopes for a cure."

"Steven is right, there is nothing more we can do, but" Michael Williams looked down at the man who had planted his seed inside of his mother, "We are only earthy physicians and we can only do so much, with God's help. But God and His Son is the great physician, and He can work miracles and complete healing on those who believe."

"Are you saying, this God, this Jesus, can heal me of this deadly virus? The same virus that took my Brook?" Eric shook his head in disbelief. "Something unseen, invisible and never heard the cries of a small child who ask Him for His help?"

"Faith is believing in something you cannot see, but you know it's real Eric. Just like the air you breathe." Steven could not understand what child his biological father was referring to, but he knew his only chance for complete healing could only come through Jesus, the Lord. Janet knew Eric was referring to himself, and she could visualize him praying for help as a tiny child and couldn't understand why God did not rescue him from his parents.

"Eric sweetheart, did you ask God to help you when you were a little boy? Maybe God did answer you but you could not see it."

"See it? Janet?" Eric took a deep breath, when he felt it getting hard to breathe. "I told you what happened, every horrible detail. Where was God's answer in that?"

"One way, God answered was through Mrs. Parks. She told you about Jesus and how to pray to him. He showed his love through her and that is why you looked forward to going to Sunday school every Sunday. She gave you hope and made you feel important." Janet touched his cold hand. "And when you reached fifteen, you said you ran away. It was God who urged you to run, even to take that money which rightfully belonged to you. Money, they had stolen from you, one way or the other, just like your mother taking your precious Bible when you were six. Perhaps, thinking everything was theirs, they took your things and sold them, even had those friends, sell or buy your things so they could get money." Janet could almost see his parents stealing his things while he was at school. "Then God sent you to the Myers family. He knew their hearts were good and they did good deeds for others. All they needed was someone who believed in Jesus and who loved them enough to tell them, like a son. You Eric, God wanted you to tell Bill and Betty about Jesus. Maybe no one took the time to share the good news with them. I think God had hoped that you would have seen them as true Christians and all they needed was someone who loved them to tell them the wonderous story how our Savior came from glory. They only needed a little push from the boy they grew to love. They had good hearts Eric, they could have learned to believe, like you did when you were six-years-old and loved going to church and being taught by Mrs. Parks, your real Christian teacher. How you learned the 23rd Psalm and inspired all your class to learn more." Janet smiled through happy tears as the truth hit her.

"You wanted to make your parents proud of you and you did! You did make your Father happy, Eric Shields, the one that really mattered. You made your Heavenly Father proud of you. He waited until you were old enough to be on your own and He sent you away from hate and danger, to a family who loved you and needed to hear His message of salvation, the message you learned as a child from a good Christian woman."

"Wow! Janet Shields, maybe you should come and give a testimony tonight." Father Benjamin had been listening in the open doorway. Her long- time friend walked over between the beds and gathered a hand from both. "Everything is ready for tonight. Three places have been reserved at the front for you, Matthew and" he patted Eric on the leg. "You, my friend. We will get you there, I promise. It is the will of God, Eric Shields, that you attend and return to His fold so you can see His salvation. My charming angelic wife will start the service with her beautiful singing, then my son and I will have words for new mothers facing the decision that could alter destiny." Zechariah's eyes twinkled. "Then Joshua will fight the battle of Lucifer and sin will come tumbling down! The sick, through Jesus, will be healed! It will be a night of miracles! Praise the Lord!"

Without another word, Zechariah Benjamin lend over and kissed Janet on her cheek and Eric on his cold forehead. He turned smiling and walked out singing softly "Just as I am, O Lamb of God, I come!"

Chapter 27

The chapel's large auditorium was filled to capacity. Chairs had been brought outside to accompany the large growing crowd that could not fit inside the church. Two large televisions monitors had been placed for easy viewing and sound so everyone could hear the great young evangelist and would not leave disappointed.

The large number of people inside and out sit quietly listening to the beautiful sound of Rebecca Bradford Benjamin, as she sang some of her favorites from her latest CD release: "The Song of Rebecca". Her angelic voice captivated the listers as their mood took on a spiritual oracle, making them feel warm and guided by the Light she sang about.

Even Eric, shaking uncontrollable under his heavy blanket, felt a strange warmth flow through his frigid body.

It was late in the spring and the night air was warm. The sky was filled with millions of twinkling stars that shown bright in the growing darkness.

Eric turn to look at Janet, who seem to be looking up at an unseen being, a beautiful smile gracing her lips. It was obvious to him that Janet felt the warmth from Rebecca's singing, as well as his son, Matthew, who had tears falling down his tan cheeks. The music went quiet and Rebecca took her seat on the large stage as her husband and son took the floor.

"Welcome brothers and sisters, to the house of the Lord! He is looking down upon us and I can feel His joy at seeing so many of His brethren among us. I feel there are some here tonight who are lost, for one reason or another. As Jesus disciples, we hope to help you find your way this very night. Sitting out there, there are those that need healing. Some of the body, some of the soul and yes, there are some who need

healing for both body and soul. You know who you are."
Joshua let his hand sweep over the people as he continued
"Among us, there are some confused women and young
girls, who are carrying a burden, unknown to those who love
them. They are too afraid to speak out, afraid of being judged.
My sisters, please know we only wish to guide you in making
the right choices under your personal circumstance. My father
has devoted his entire life on this very subject, so I will turn
the program over to him now. Ladies, as well as gentlemen,
Father Zechariah Benjamin and Sister Anne Marie.

"Where do babies come from?" Father Benjamin smiled
as laughter rose from the audience. "Yes, we know how a baby
is put in place and is started, but my question was, where do
they come from in the first place! I know you might say, I get
what you mean. God created women to have babies and be
called mothers." Everyone clapped and with a big smile, he
continued. "Yes, that is also true, but not the answer I'm after.
Babies start out in Heaven." There was a surprised gasp from
those listening.

"Hard to believe? God can and does create everything and
everyone. A baby is created one at a time, in the form of a tiny
soul. In Heaven, God can see this baby as well as the angels
who stand by waiting. Waiting to receive the baby and be put
in charge of its well- being, to guard and guide him or her,
throughout their time on earth. Thus, your guardian angel!"
Again, joyful laughter and clapping arose from the large
crowd.

"The baby can also see Heaven, along with the angels and
Jesus, our Lord and Savior. This precious little person is God's
special gift to one lucky set of parents. God means for these
parents to love, teach, and nourish this child until it is fully
grown so he or she will become what the Lord has planned for
them." Zechariah looked around at all the confused faces and
he smiled. "Let me share with you a true story about a young
couple who had a little boy and a brand- new baby girl. The

parents worried that their son was jealous over his baby sister just by his actions toward her and by the way he was always watching her. One evening after laying the baby down in its crib, they noticed their little boy slip into her bedroom where she was laying. Not sure of their son's intentions, they watched just outside the door and heard the little boy talking to his baby sister. The young parents were amazed at what they heard. The young boy was asking his baby sister to remind him what Heaven was like, because he was forgetting." Zechariah saw genuine tears from the audience and several young women were actually weeping.

"I know it feels like your entire life has been ruined if you get pregnant by mistake and your thoughts turn to abortion. Many people will have you to believe it is alright to abort a baby in the first term or two, but my dear sisters, from the moment that seed was sown, that very little soul was place inside that tiny baby and it was alive and God's special gift." Father Benjamin's eyes were filled with passion because he could see the pain these women were feeling.

"I know you feel like a victim, maybe you've even been raped. I have two raped victims here today who will testify that they were faced with the same problem you are facing and the choices they made and how it affected the rest of their life. Remember my sisters, before you take this baby's life, it too is a victim. It is helpless, depending on its mother to protect he or she until they can take care of their own life. At this time, I will turn the program over to four women who have been in your shoes. Zech sat down as Rebecca and Sister Anne, along with Victoria and Regina walked to the front of the stage. Eric felt like crawling under his seat and would have if he had felt up to it. He felt sure they would not point him out though.

"Sisters in Christ, my name is Sister Anne. I was a rape victim many years ago and found myself pregnant by a complete stranger at fifteen-years-old. Growing up in the Catholic faith, I went to confession so my priest could offer me some advice as to what I should do. Like Father Benjamin, my priest told me that the baby I carried was as much a victim as I was and it was only right for me to have the baby, then put it up for adoption. I did have my baby, a son and named him Zech. My loving parents raised him as their own son, and now my son, Father Zechariah Benjamin and I make it our calling to save God's innocent babies."

Another surprised gasp came from the large crowd from the nun's revelation about the priest they all admired. Then Rebecca stepped up and there was complete silence.

"I too was raped, my dear friends, at my home, in the dark, by a man who knew a lot about me and many men that I was acquainted with. Good men with families, from church, from my local drug store, my college professor, and my own father and our hired help on the farm. The rapist threw suspicion on each one of them so I could not guess which one had done the evil act. It did end up being one of those men but I can tell you this day, I have forgiven him completely. I forgave him the day my beautiful son was born. The seed had been sown and my little boy became one of God's special gifts. He is Joshua Benjamin!" an even bigger gasp came from the audience when Rebecca revealed her son's name. After taking her seat, Regina and Victoria stepped forward.

"Unlike Sister Anne and our dear friend Rebecca, I was having an affair with the man I loved at the time. The affair brought forth a son but my lover wanted no part of it. I am happy I chose to keep my son, one of God's special gifts. If it hadn't been for my son, the deadly Verta Virus might not have a cure today, as well as other important discoveries. Praise God Steven lives, thousands have been saved because of his God given talent." Victoria smiled over at Regina as she could tell the people were astonished by these revelations from the news anchor they all loved and admired. The audience also wondered how this last woman could add to the important men saved from a simple choice.

"My name is Regina. Many of you may know me as the head nurse at Mercy Hospital and Maglen Hospital, as well as councilor for both. What you do not know is my previous occupation. I was working at Sadie's Ladies." A huge reaction came from the listeners as mothers covered their young children's ears, bringing a smile on Regina's face. "There is no need to worry dear mothers, I will not state what I did there. I think most of you can guess what I did for a living." Regina laughed along with the crowd. "I have been forgiven, believe me. Sadie's Ladies is where I met and fell in love with one of my clients who sewed the seed inside me and I found myself pregnant and thinking seriously about another abortion." Again, the crowd gave a surprised gasp.

"Yes, I killed one of God's special gifts. A sweet innocent little girl who came to me in a dream and ask me to save her brother, Michael, the baby I was carrying. So, Doctor Michael Marshall Williams was born and many of you know he is one of the leading sought- after surgeons in the United States." A clap echoed through the church and outside the opened doors. "Yes, he too, is a special gift from God."

Father Benjamin joined his wife and mother as Michael, Steven, and Joshua stepped out next to their mothers. The audience exploded in loud applause and Zechariah raised his hands.

This next part will be very difficult for most everyone present, but it must be told. Doctor Michael Williams and Doctor Steven Spilman will now come forward to share the next part of our program.

"My brother Steven and I are both physicians. We are privy to certain medical facts the general public are not aware of. These true facts we are going to share with you will be hard to hear. As we bring to light the real truth concerning how abortions are performed and how God's innocent babies are murdered. With this crusade being televised throughout America and other countries, we decided now was the time for everyone to know these horrible details.

Stage 1: Cut open the uterus, then cut up the fetus and scrape it out. All this is performed while the fetus is alive.

Stage 2: The doctor puts a huge needle in and sucks out the baby. As the live baby is being sucked out, it comes apart."

Steven walked up to the mic. "This doesn't get any easier, but it must be told.

Stage 3: The doctor sticks a needle into a woman's abdomen when the baby is 6 to 7 months. That is full term. The doctor sucks out the fluid that feeds the baby and replaces it with a poison salt solution. The innocent baby burns up inside as its skin turns black. It suffers for one hour before it dies.

Stage 4: The doctor delivers the live baby and uses it for experiments, taking pieces of it organs until they finally kill the baby by thrusting a knife in their little heart.

There wasn't a dry eye in the audience when the doctors finished their description of how abortions were performed. Michael looked out, tears running down his cheeks as he concluded with

"If you are considering abortion, please pray about it and remember, this baby you are carrying is God's special child." Michael and Steven joined their mothers as Father Benjamin stood back up.

"At the close of the service, all those ladies wishing to get help from us, please come forward during the last hymn. We will be waiting on the left side of the stage to help all who will come. God bless you and remember, I AM GOD'S VOICE calling out, SAVE MY BABIES!"

The clapping did not stop until the group took their seats and Reverend Joshua Benjamin walked to the center of the stage. He lifted up his voice and said "LET THE HEALLING BEGIN!"

Chapter 28

"One word on behalf of God's babies, the Holy Bible says in Psalm 139:13: 'You created my inmost being, you knit me together in my mother's womb!'"

There are some of you searching for truth tonight. Maybe you feel lost and alone. Maybe you feel God has let you down or has not heard you when you called out to Him. My friends, believe me when I say, you are never alone. God hears EVERYTHING you say, whether you are praising Him or shouting at Him with hate in your heart. There is no word, no thought you have made, that has not been heard by the Almighty God!

"Maybe, instead of blaming him, that which is perfect and makes no mistakes, you should look to your own actions. Go back and ask yourself, what choices did I make to get where I am at. Not what God has done, but what you did to find yourself into the bad situation you have found yourself in." Joshua looked out over the silent group of people as his words set in.

"If you believe, and I mean truly believe, you will start to hear God's voice. You may not be able to hear Him from without, but truly, if you are sincere in your belief, you can and will hear Him from within. Within your heart and your soul.

How does one hear from their heart or soul, you may be asking? It is simple. It is called FAITH! A belief in a Savior who can speak to you in spirit. When you believe in the Lord Jesus, you will receive the Holy Spirit, that third part of the Holy Trinity that comes from God, our creator and Holy Father, Jesus Christ, our risen Lord and Savior!

It is not as hard as one might think to receive Jesus Christ into their life. All you have to do is ask Him. Ask Him to forgive your sins, accept Him as your Lord and Savior, the Son of the Almighty God and you will be excepted by the one who leads to life eternal!" Joshua stepped to the edge of the big stage to get close to the people and he looked around at the many individual faces.

"If your body is broken, if you are sick, cripple, blind or carry the deadly virus inside you, that hopes to claim your life for Lucifer, defy him. Come forward and let the hand of Jesus, the Great Physician, touch you and heal you and make you alive and well again through Him!" Joshua attention fell on his real father, sitting pale and shaking on the front row.

"You only need to have faith, my friends and dear ones. Faith no bigger than a grain of mustard seed. To become healed, you only need to believe on the one who can make you well, Jesus, the Savior. The gift of life only your Savior can grant you and all you need is to step forward and give your life to Him. Its really just that simple. He's waiting with more love than you ever felt possible. Come my brothers, come my sisters, my mothers and." Joshua's eyes fell on Eric "Come, my fathers! Come give your life to the Lord, Jesus Christ, and He will make you whole!"

The music began to play as Rebecca led the choir in singing "Come, come, come, to Jesus, He will heal your soul. Come, come, come, to Jesus, you are safe in His fold."

The people started filing forward, both from inside the church and many sitting outside. There were eight women who made their way to the left side of the stage, six in their twenties to thirties and two young teenagers. Father Benjamin, Sister Anne, Regina, and Victoria were there to pray with them and offer future help. A cripple man came forward in his wheelchair as a blind -women was helped up to the altar by a good friend. Eric stood up on trembling legs as Janet and Matthew jumped up to support him and help get up to the altar through the growing crowd. When they finally made it, Eric noticed the cripple man was standing up as tears of joy ran

143

down his face as he gave praises to the Lord for healing him at Joshua's touch through the name of Jesus. Eric's tears made it hard to see the blind woman standing in front of his son as he heard Joshua's strong voice call out

"In the name of Jesus, you are made whole!"

The woman blinked her tears away and turned to see her close friend for the first time. Her smile was radiant as she proclaimed "I can see! Mary Jo, I can see you my dear friend! Praise the Lord! Thank you, Jesus!" she shouted with complete happiness.

Joshua saw his father and motioned for Janet and Matthew to step away. He made eye contact with him and ask

"Father, come to me and tell me what you want." Eric choked up as he moved forward.

"I...I want to know Jesus again. I want Him to forgive me for all my many sins and..." his tears began to flow. "to be healed so I can become a better man, a better father, to all my sons and" he looked at Janet who was also crying, "to be a better husband to my darling devoted wife."

"There is one more thing, is there not sir?" Joshua had tears in his eyes, knowing that God had finally gotten through to His little lost boy.

"I want to see my Brook again!" Eric cried. "I'm sorry Lord! I was lost! I believe in you Jesus with all my heart and I'm not just saying this because I am sick and only want to be cured. If I die now, I know I will see you Lord Jesus, just like I did when I was a baby in Heaven. I just thank you Lord for giving Rebecca, Regina, Victoria, and my dear wife Janet, the strength and love to have these special babies you gave us." Tears flooded his eyes as he wept uncontrollable. "I'm sorry I tried to destroy these special babies, who grew up to save me from certain death and hell. I'm sorry for ruining my darling Brook's life. For making her deny you when I know how much she truly loved you, Lord. For not letting her be my one and only love and for forbidding her to have any children when I know she would have made a wonderful mother. And mostly, for being the one responsible for her early death, by my wrong choice in going to that house of prostitution when I had the best thing waiting for me. For the man she loved so much she gave her life for me and put up with my many affairs! Why, why was I so blind, not to see what I had was all I needed. And I used my perfect wonderful wife the same. I was deeply in love with these two women and I hurt them both not to mention hurting Regina, Victoria, and sweet innocent Rebecca.

Eric dropped to his knees "Mostly, I hurt you, my Lord! I became an Atheist and denied that you even existed! I am the worse kind of sinner and yet I believe my Jesus will forgive me for all my scarlet sins! His loving mercy will save me and set me free to believe again and tell others of His salvation."

"The Lord who hears all has heard our confession Eric Shields. You are forgiven and through the name of Jesus Christ, you are made whole, both in body and in soul!"

Chapter 29

High on a mountain top, overshadowing the small town of Maglen, set an old white farmhouse. Abraham Chadumn had been saying his nightly prayers as was his custom for ninety-seven years, ever since he was two-years-old. If he lived till Easter he would make it to his 100th birthday. Being a true man of faith, old Abraham had always thanked the good Lord for giving him another year to pray for others.

He had heard on the news about the deadly virus and all the poor sinners who had died before the God gifted young scientist, Doctor Steven Spilman had discovered the cure. Abraham regretted the fact that he could not go down to the small town to hear the young evangelist in person. He never missed a single Broadcast on his great crusades given all over the world. He admired the gifted young minister who had come to preach salvation and to heal those who were afflicted. After all, Abraham was 99 years-old, almost 100. He was losing his hearing and eyesight, but never the flame that burnt within his soul.

After hearing about Mr. Chadumn from his mother and father, Joshua Benjamin paid Abraham a visit upon his arrival to Maglen. They had a lengthy discussion about the Holy scriptures, on faith and hope for all mankind because of the great sacrifice Jesus had made for our sins when He laid down His life upon a Roman cross, over 2,000 years ago. Old Abraham had expressed his gratitude to the young preacher for coming to Maglen and offering hope and healing.

Joshua Benjamin was impressed with the old man of great faith and praised him for his faithful prayer life that had lifted many a soul from despair.

Before Joshua departed, he said a prayer for Abraham and touched his eyes and ears, asking the good Lord to heal his servant and grant him a long life, so he might continue his service to the Almighty God!

Now looking out into the moonless night adorned with twinkling stars, the dark night sky seemed to part, like a veil on one bright spot below the mountain. The glow that was flowing out, then up, was coming from one spot, one place. Abraham smiled, because he knew it was coming from the chapel, which was filled with the light of God.

Abraham's old pale eyes could see plainly the glow grow brighter and brighter, and he could visualize all the many souls being saved and the power of the Holy Spirit filling each saved person with the flamed spirit of light.

The old man's lips smiled as he began to quote scripture, the words of Jesus.

"YOU ARE THE LIGHT OF THE WORLD! A CITY SET ON A HILL CANNOT BE HID. NETHER DO MEN LIGHT A CANDLE, AND PUT IT UNDER A BUSHEL, BUT PUT IN ON A CANDLESTICK; AND GIVETH LIGHT UNTO ALL THAT IS IN THE HOUSE!" Abraham smiled as he continued to quote the Lord.

"LET YOUR LIGHT SO SHINE BEFORE MEN, THAT THEY MAY SEE YOUR GOOD DEEDS AND GLORIFY YOUR FATHER WHICH IS IN HEAVEN!"

The old man's eyes glistened with the tears of peace and total joy, as he watched the soft glow growing even more brilliant. His voice rang out

"The Holy Spirit has filled each heart with the spirit of light, so that the spirit of Christ can shine through. Bless be to God! The lost have been found and the sick have been made whole and the goodness of the Lord giveth light unto 'all' that are in the chapel!

Abraham's ears were opened up as he could hear the voice of an angel's song. "Just as I am, O Lamb of God, I come, I come!"

Chapter 30

Eric felt the same warm glow he had witness when he was six-years-old after hearing his teacher say

"Eric, your Father in Heaven is proud of you!"

Through happy tears, Eric Shields looked up at the cross that hung in front of the altar. With a strong voice, he released the words of the 23rd Psalm. He didn't just memorize it, but had kept it imbedded deep within his heart for many years.

"THE LORD IS MY SHEPHERD; I SHALL NOT WANT. HE MAKETH ME LIE DOWN IN GREEN PASTURES: HE LEADETH ME BESIDE THE STILL WATERS. HE RESTORETH MY SOUL: HE LEADETH ME IN THE PATHS OF RIGHTEOUSNESS FOR HIS NAME SAKE."

As Eric lifted up the holy words in the divine presence of the Almighty God, Janet and Regina glanced at each other as tears of happiness danced in their eyes. They knew the lost six-year-old boy had finally found his way back home.

"YEH, THOUGH I WALK TROUGH THE VALLEY OF SHADOW OF DEATH, I WILL FEAR NO EVIL; FOR THOU ART WITH ME; THY ROD AND THY STAFF THEY COMFORT ME. THOU PREPAREST A TABLE BEFORE ME IN THE PRESENCE OF MINE ENIMIES; THOU ANNOINTEST MY HEAD WITH OIL; MY CUP RUNETH OVER. SURELY GOODNESS AND MERCY SHALL FOLLOW ME ALL THE DAYS OF MY LIFE: AND I WILL DWELL IN THE HOUSE OF THE LORD FOREVER."

The tears from the people of Maglen were flowing that night for Professor Eric Shields. Many of his past and present students were in attendance and listened in stunned silence to his confession of all his many sins. Sins with a big variety of women, wanting unborn babies to be aborted for his own personal desires and his selfishness for lust. The sin for leading his impressionable students to think his way, by telling them there was no God and that God was a myth, a fairy tale, a beautiful story but mere fiction. The students listened to the man they had all believed and looked up too. Now, their professor was suddenly turning his views completely around. Eric caught many of their puzzled faces and sensed their questions and their disappointment. Without consciously thinking about his actions, he picked up the microphone and began to talk.

"If any of my students are listening, both past and present students from Maglen University, my task tonight is to reverse the damage I have done and start telling you the real facts. God is not dead! God is very much alive and real. I was the one that was dead. I had let people in my past kill my faith in Jesus and without Him, I was dead, both inside and out, so the devil found me easy to get. But, I have been reborn this night and I can say without a single doubt, God is alive! He lives as He has since the beginning of time, as we know it, and far beyond that! God does not need us, my friends, but we need God!" Eric looked out with compassion.

"God loves us so much, He gave the one thing He cherished most in all His creation, His Son, His beautiful Son! So, God sent Jesus to earth in the form of a baby, to live and grow among everyday people, like you and me. Jesus knew what it was like to feel joy, grief, and pain.

Working with his earthy father Joseph, Jesus knew what it was like to work long hours. He knew rough callous hands, aching muscles and a tired back from lifting and stooping. His feet and legs grew tired after traveling the dusty roads by foot, day after day. I am certain his head had to ache with the Scribes and Pharisees following His every move and giving Him threats at every turn or good deed done. Having to put up with twelve grown men who acted more like children at times

149

and asking far too many questions when they should have known the messages meanings after being with Him so long.

Being humiliated in front of a great number of people for doing His Father's will. The agony of pulling a heavy Roman cross after being beaten mercilessly with a Roman whip at Pilot's command. Then the terrific agonizing pain of being nailed through his hands and feet on the very cross he was forced to carry down the narrow streets of Jerusalem all the way to Golgotha, the hill called Calvary. And if that were not enough for the man to bear, the soldiers gram a crown of sharp thorns down over his head!" Tears made it hard for Eric to see the audience, but he felt compelled to go on.

"Our loving God sent His, only Son, Jesus, to this earth for this purpose. To become the sacrificial lamb. The perfect lamb without blemish, without sin. To carry all the sins every committed or will be committed, inside Him on that cross and die on that cross to take away the sins of the world, so that we may be made alive through Him!

Jesus, our Savior, went through all that pain for us and all He ask in return is that we believe in Him. Ask forgiveness for your sins and do the will of His Father." Eric's eyes had been focused on the big cross that hung on the chapel wall. He turned to face the crowd who had been silently listening to his testimony.

"Most of you here are Christian people and you know Jesus arose from the cold grave, just as He said. Now He has returned to the Father where He lives and waits for His people to join Him in Heaven." Eric searched the crowd until he saw Janet and Regina, holding hands like old friends instead of wife and mistress. "I recently asked two very wise women this question: If Jesus is so good and filled with love, why wouldn't I see my very good friends Bill and Betty in Heaven if I go there? I had told them how Bill and Betty had taken me into their home and hearts when I had run away at fifteen from bad 'Christian' parents. I informed them about this beautiful couple giving needy people whatever they needed and showing kindness to everyone. They never met a stranger and they loved all people, but they were unbelievers.

Then I was told, unless they believe in Jesus, I would not see them there." Eric smiled down at the two ladies, who despite their past circumstances, they were now friends. "I know what they were trying to tell me. When you learn to put your full trust in Jesus and truly believe in Him, the truth is revealed. No matter how many good deeds you do, it will not get you into Heaven. You can never save yourself on your own. Jesus said: 'No one comes to the Father but by me!' Jesus also said: "Whosoever liveth and believeth in me, shall NEVER DIE!' Just believe!

My friends, Heaven is not in a galaxy far away! Heaven is truly just a breath away. You can reach out your hand and know Jesus will touch you, it is that close. The woman I loved most, slipped from this world to her Heavenly home right before my eyes. I could not smell the veil opening for her, but my son Joshua could. He could sense the angels drawing near. I could not see the angels coming to take my loved one away, but my Brook could." Eric took a deep breath as he remembered just what he had seen. "But what I did see my friends, was a glow on my Brook's beautiful face. A peace that radiated over her entire body and I could tell her pain had vanished. She asked me to kiss her one last time." Eric choked up, his tears falling from his green eyes as he could still see her face. "As I kissed my darling's lips, I felt her take her last breath as she slipped from my embrace into the loving arms of Jesus, our Savior. With a glad heart I can say, I know this day, I will see my Brook again because the love of Jesus saved me!"

Eric looked out over the large group of people and seeing their tears, he felt moved even more.

"I ask all of you to forgive me, for leading you astray but it is never too late to turn your life around. Just look at me!

My lustful life had me in the valley of the shadow of death, but the Holy Spirit broke through this hard- shell Satan had placed around me when I was a small boy. Thanks to my son, who was not aborted by his loving Christian mother, Joshua's words, given to him by the Holy Spirit, touched my very soul and melted my doubting heart." Eric touched his chest as he closed his eyes,

"The Lord has given me a chance to live, a chance to finish my journey on this earth, beside my beautiful forgiving wife, Janet and my son, Matthew, of whom I will show more love than even he might want."

Matthew smiled broadly as the audience laughed softly through their tears.

"And I will love and pray for the fine works of my other three sons, Michael, Steven and Joshua, whose love and care went way beyond anything I had ever received from my own parents, even though I did not deserve their love and care. I can see it in their heart that they have forgiven me as have their beautiful mothers. I will be forever grateful and strive to make you proud to call me your second father. I would never try to replace those dedicated men who raised you, Zachariah, Todd, and Eli."

Eric suddenly realized he had been preaching and taking up Joshua's time. He turned to face the young evangelist and smiled sheepishly as he handed him the microphone. The smiled that radiated over the young minister's face was brilliant as he took the mic.

"That was quite a sermon father!" Joshua winked at a blushing Eric and turned to the people and said "Can I hear an AMEN!"

"AMEN!" the voices resonated in unison as Joshua held out his arms.

"Go in peace, hope, and love! Remember the words of our Lord Jesus. LET YOU LIGHT SHINE BEFORE MEN, THAT THEY MAY SEE YOUR GOOD WORKS AND

GLORIFY YOUR FATHER, WHICH IS IN HEAVEN! AMEN!"

Eric Shields walked out of that chapel on that warm spring night with his family, a changed man. He let Jesus back in his heart and his light would shine through in his new chosen vocation, professor of religion at Duke University. Eric would always have Brook in his heart and knew he would see her again. In his heart, he hoped Billy and Betty had found Jesus and he would see them again, along with his own parents, of whom he finally forgave.

Eight young women had walked inside the chapel that night and were pondering whether or not to have an abortion. Eight women walked out of the chapel that night, feeling the love and compassion of their risen Lord and a new- found love for the innocent gift God had given them.

Many lost souls were found that night in the small town of Maglen. Even those Christians who already believed had a new awakening.

The night gave way to morning, but the glow of God's love brightened up the cool spring morning. Easter was coming again!"

JOAN BYRD

AUTHOR'S NOTES

Patrick, my guardian angel shared with me the words to the Christmas carol Rebecca was chosen to sing in her Christmas cantata titled: "Mary Had a Little Lamb"

"The Little Lamb"

Mary had a little lamb, one dark cold Christmas morn
Mary named him Jesus when her little lamb was born.

Mary laid him in a manger, while she watched him sleep,
a little babe, the son of God, slept with the stable sheep.

Mary had a little lamb, a gift from god above.
Mary's heart was full of joy, her heart was full of love!

Mary's perfect little lamb lit up the cradle stall.
He would be the altar lamb, who died to save us all.

Mary had a little lamb, god's perfect holy child,
who left his home in heaven, to live with us a while.

Written by:
Joan Byrd
&
told by:
my loving guardian angel
Patrick

ABOUT THE AUTHOR

Joan Bodsford Byrd was born and raised on a farm in Winston-Salem, North Carolina. Her parents were Lindsay 'Tip' Bodsford and Garnette 'Dot' Vogler Bodsford. She is the fifth child of six daughters and she and her five sisters have always been close to one another.

Joan was brought up in the Methodist faith and she still is an active member of the same church she attended as a small child. God blessed Joan with the gift of singing and she joined the adult choir at the young age of twelve. Having the gift of drama, Joan has written and acted in several church dramas, such as: "Jesus of Nazareth", "Two from Galilee" and along with a youth group played the part of Robin in "Godspell", where she: sang "day by day"

Joan taught fifth and six grade Sunday school for almost twenty years, starting at around 18-years-old. She loved teaching the children and always received as much as she gave. It was a blessing she will always cherish.

Joan had the gift of art and loved to draw and paint. One art critic said her paintings were very much like Grandma Moses. When she taught Sunday school, Joan drew Jesus and the twelve disciples, plus all our biblical ancestors, from Adam & Eve.

Joan has been married to her loving husband, Ray Byrd for 32 years and she has been blessed with her very best friend, guardian, guide, and the very best storyteller known to man! Patrick, God's beautiful gifted & loving angel!!!

Bless This Little Child, Lord

—Unknown Author

Lord, look down from heaven above
And touch this special child with love.
Protect and guide this little one
Till each and every day is done:
Remind us often that it's true:
This little life is a gift from you.
A miracle you've sent our way!
Lord, bless this little child today.

www.ingramcontent.com/pod-product-compliance
Lightning Source LLC
Chambersburg PA
CBHW060351180626
46817CB00008B/2972

* 9 7 8 1 6 3 0 6 6 5 0 3 6 *